D1363664

BIRDSWIM FISHFLY

BIRDSWIM FISHFLY

Gayathri Prabhu

Rupa & Co

Typeset in Weiss by
Nikita Overseas Pvt. Ltd.
1410 Chiranjiv Tower
43 Nehru Place
New Delhi 110 019

Printed in India by
Saurabh Printers Pvt. Ltd.
A-16 Sector-IV
Noida 201 301

I'm nobody! Who are you?
Are you nobody, too?
Then there's a pair of us — don't tell!
They'd banish us, you know.

— EMILY DICKINSON

flowers and daughters

1

IT IS NEEDLESS TO PRESUME THAT ONE NEEDS TO PAINT TO be a painter or write verse to be a poet but almost unavoidable in the perception of the world. Very often have symphonies composed and played themselves to an ecstatic stupor in my head though nobody calls me a musician. Yet I am. An artist with a dire lack of art.

My story starts here, not from any grand design or wily lures of a plot. I have no such pretensions. It flatters my feeble mind to start from the uncertain, a misty nook known only to the wind but the path to which is locked in my heart and the keys flung into some bottomless misery far from heaven. Hell! It is pathetic how people write about everything they can scrape off the bottom of shoes not long after walking in the muck of lives, theirs and others. I make no promises that this one is any different. But it might interest those who for no particular reason are deciding to read on, that this somnolent morning I am struck by a thought: the only reason I have not been discovered as a genius by the world is because I simply haven't tried my hand at it.

It is that languid hour following lunch when the mind is content and the grounds of the Big House are evacuated by the summer sun. The sheet seems endless space for the subject chosen, a little bush with white flowers, star-like with their five pointed petals. Ambition knows its limitations and is willing to make a prudent start. The little bottle of water comes unscrewed to invite the four brushes to settle in. A dwarfed pencil is poised between bent fingers. A bush has never been more daunting. I have taken a thousand walks by this little piece of foliage, alone and with company, each time smiling at the simplicity of its existence, the sparseness of its blooms. It is now the turn of the bush to have its own laugh.

I find myself under a tree that is suitable in every way. Standing demurely, far apart from the forceful building, its broad juicy leaves glitter on the surface while knitting diligent cool patterns of shade on the grass below. I crouch under it. The four paintbrushes sticking out of my pocket have been borrowed from the twins and cannot be lost from carelessness. There are enough teeth imprints on the edge of each handle for impeccable identification. I can only chew off more to prove they are mine or someone else's. It is much easier to simply put them to use before returning in good faith.

This is a terrible burden, this effort and indecisiveness, this having to paint one's first painting with another's brushes. I have already spent a good ten minutes gazing at the brushes in hope of acquaintance. The paints offer some consolation for they are my own, dried and cracked from disuse since school, dusty too from being forgotten in the clutter of my closet for many years. Surely I must have painted as a child – why else would I retain a paint-box among my cluttered possessions? – but oddly, it is hard to find one lucid memory when I let the paint, wet and nebulous, drop upon a sheet of paper, to flood into any shape that I conspired to colour. For long I have been an artist without a single painting bearing my name. I am now ready to change that.

The elementary sketch is easy enough. The shape suggesting the bush is rather recognisable and the flowers, though slightly distorted, continue to hang on to the parent form. Colours are to be my undoing: the green is unwieldy and the white, non-committal. The brushes are obstinate monsters and the paint is too chapped to flow. Imagination has come across its first stumbling block. Form hates texture and hues are sniggering at shades, fingers not having learnt the first thing about deciphering the creative vision in my chest. The blob of green with greyish-white holes on my sheet of paper is easily described. Disgusting. So when the tea bell tolls merrily in the distance, all I have managed are tears in my eyes and murky water in the bottle.

I start digging a hole not far from the bush, shove both the paper and the old paint-box in it and neatly pack the mud back in. The brushes, I carefully wipe on my socks and stick them back in my pocket. On their return depends a friendship. As for the bottle, I place it carefully on the grass and kick it with all my might. It meekly launches into flight and lands at the far end of the lawn. A relief! The bottle has somehow had it worse than me today.

I clearly am a painter who cannot paint. And how bad can that be? The paintings will continue to breathe to life inside me and stay there — trembling with passion, flushed with tender charm, throbbing from excessive beauty – or better still, fade away for lack of space in a shrivelled memory. I console myself. My images, free from the bondage of being defined, will have the exclusive privilege of being seen by only one person – me. That is something I can live with, live for. However tea in the evenings is not to be missed for any reason, not even for art. I walk back slowly towards the white building.

2

THEY ALWAYS PUT THEIR HEADS TOGETHER WHEN THEY laughed. His merriment gushing out first, gruff but kind; hers soft, tinkling its way through the summer air. They were happy, Maria and the boy who worked in the milk booth down the street, swollen with a love they pretended did not exist.

We would walk in hurried excited steps to the canopy theatre that fluttered over an empty plot not too far from the house. I would always walk a step ahead, an accomplice in that pretence, trying to leave behind the raw ardour they oozed so recklessly. I bought my own ticket and sat alone in the row ahead of them, close enough to be supervised but far enough to be ignored. The few other customers who bothered to drag their feet out on those steamy afternoons never bothered with me, perhaps repelled by my clumsy appearance, mostly accomplished by hair cut so short that it struggled to cover my scalp. The rest of the effect was achieved by clothes that my brothers had outgrown, for it was yet unknown to me that I could still retain my girlhood in them.

I whistled with the other boys and loudly roared at ludicrous jokes I did not understand. Behind me, Maria sat with the boy, both making the strangest noises while I watched the screen riveted. They found each other in darkness and I discovered both a shadowy world of stories and a way to escape my irksome brothers for hours. Any inconveniences the young lovers must have felt on account of my tagging along on their jaunts was redeemed by my diplomatic silences whenever Ma discovered our absence from the house. I was less a child, more an alibi. If prodded too much, I insisted we went no further than the park because my parents, if they had the authority, were the sorts who would happily burn every strip of celluloid in the world. They simply did not believe in entertainment in the guise of a flickering light on a dusty white sheet under some dingy blue canopy.

If truth be told, it was not as if the young couple loved my company. I think I more than once spied Maria's young man make a noose out of any stray rope he found on the pavement and tiptoe behind me, feigning to be a hangman. He was rather morbid, now that I think of it, and he had the grimiest brown teeth I had ever seen.

A year later, when Maria left our house with a stomach that brought her shame, he is said to have hanged himself from the roof of the milk booth, one warm humid afternoon when the shutters were pulled down. I missed them both. They always laughed together, and even when Maria got upset enough to call him 'a fat monkey', they cried in chorus.

3

THERE WAS FATHER, STERN AND PERPETUALLY TIRED-LOOKING, bent over a cluttered wooden desk, nibbling on the little finger of his left hand for concentration. There was mother, her thick glasses arresting the outdoor splendour in the confines of the same room, her fingers gripped around a flying pen that raised its head only to hop to the next line. There were brothers, herded around a low rickety table, cramming their school lessons in chants. And there was Maria, walking in and out with two cups of tea, one dark and sweet, the other brown and bitter, her skirt a burst of floral patterns.

There was also me, sitting on the narrow window ledge, my feet sticking out through two rods in the iron grill and pushed far enough for toes to graze over the yellow dahlias that grandmother prizes above all.

From my perch, I see my grandmother in the garden, the only one to escape all the rules that our parents took much effort to lay down each day, approaching the window with an overweight aluminium watering-can. I had a flash of an instant to withdraw my feet, which I was confident of doing, till the panicky discovery of finding them immobile. There was then that shut room – the relief of rescue so brief that it is not worth mentioning – and my mother's hand turning the cane around to avoid hurt to herself when it came down forcefully on my flesh.

The iron had to be cut to prise out my stuck legs. I had not meant to cause trouble but that is apparently all I had ever caused my parents since they blundered their way to my birth – a fact that had been yelled and repeated in the hours following the incident. I was grateful to be left alone in my room for the rest of the day.

It was not till I saw the sky outside the window thicken into a late dusk that I dared to try the door handle. It was unlocked. Maria watching black and white flashes on the television had turned it to its highest volume, but amplification still being a primitive affair then, the echoes in the house were like dull thuds. It also implied that the house was empty but for the two of us. I inched into the drawing room and turned stiff midway. On a side table, sitting in an ugly brown ceramic vase and drooping over from lack of strength, were three yellow dahlias. It was the perfect ornament for an austere home and I have never hated anything as much.

4

THERE IS NOW THIS HOUSE AND THERE IS ME IN IT.

The Big House melts into the mist so many times each day that it is impossible to predict when it stays whole. In the noon light, it stands as a block of cement. Grim. Again now in the evenings, with the mountains sighing big clouds over our heads, the walls turn pale, translucent pale. The doors slam shut in respect to the soup that the cook stirs as it boils, rises, spills over, till there is almost nothing else to smell. Only the narrow open window in my room battles the familiar fumes as I stand at it to watch a patch of purple wild flowers. Having exhausted a lifetime in one trifle trot of the sun across the sky, the flowers slowly drop into the grass, petal after petal, in deference for the night. It is a ritualistic funeral that can only be washed away by the fresh brood of colour awakened by a new day's sunshine. Usually I watch them with indifferent attentiveness. Today I am sad, a little humbled by the battle of the bush, my pride wrung hard and put out to dry.

I nibble on a stale biscuit lying forgotten in the drawer. Have you noticed how there is just too much sadness in the air? Intangible and invisible, the barely audible groan of the human spirit that unfailingly hangs over our heads. There is little meaning to all we do and so little do we understand. How can anyone ever lay claim to happiness? How do we manage to survive just so that we can die? How?

If indeed it is inescapable to have an identity, I was reasonably convinced that the one of an artist does me justice. But that was before I had to reckon with the bush. I could have been any of those many things my parents offered to dream for me. They were admirable, the parents who spelt out their vision for a clumsy bed-wetting baby. Respectable professions like being a doctor or a government clerk were high on the list. If they knew then that I would opt to be a free-ranging artist with not a single sketch deserving of a frame or a poet who cannot think of two lines of verse that can amicably stand together, would they have smothered me with a pillow? Possibly. I will certainly recommend it for any child with the same future in sight. Make no mistakes – this is a wretched life.

And yet I am cooped up in this house. Why? Another joke of the human situation, if you please. Nobody knows. No, not the ones who manage the Big House or the three burly brothers who drove me here or my parents who are in the company of the dead and hence least likely to care about the inexplicable little irritants of living that continue to inflict us. I do know the part of the story that I am supposed to – I am here because I was meant to.

Isn't it repulsive how we simplify the human lot? There always has to be a fire exit, an escape chute – if God does not absolve us when we crawl with true penitence, then karma will ensure that patient endurance is rewarded some ten births down the line, all that I have clearly declared feed for the birds.

I don't mean to complain. Life here is very liveable. The meals arrive with delightful predictability: no small talk, no fancy cutlery to handle daintily, just good wholesome food served on the dot. What more could a soul want? If I am told there is something more enticing than a timely meal (apart from the artistic throes), I will dutifully snigger in the face of the bearer of such tidings.

The twins will agree to the happiness of an uneventful life – no school and as many hours of painting as they wish. They are little artists on a mission, fighting empty space with their pencils and erasers. I was in a few of those paintings myself, a midget with yellow streaming hair. I am tall and my hair is as black as black can be. I am also a woman and it does not matter that they think otherwise, straightening my body into hard masculine lines. The twins have one rule they never break. They only draw on walls. Was my artistic bout born from seeing ten-year-old boys stick their fingers in paint? I have asked myself that too. Who is to say?

One predominant thought has survived the last few months and I now realise it to have been misleading. To explain, I will have to hop, skip and dive through time, both the recent and the long past, to all those days when my existence was in anticipation of this one. If not a painter, maybe a writer, perhaps a dancer, or even a bird on a tree. My chest aches, for a wasted day, a wasted lifetime.

Forget the artist! Where is the art? Nowhere. I do not exist. I am in the penumbra region, swaddled in twilight, the womb of neither-this-nor-that. And I cry to be born.

5

NANI DIED SOON AFTER THOSE DAHLIAS DID. SHE WAS THE mother of my mother and did not appear to have passed on much of herself. Ma prided on being all that she was not. Nani knew enough of the English alphabet to read 'the cat on the mat' from my text books but said that she did not care much for fancy 'phoren' education. Ma would always sigh her disagreement for she had put in many-many years at many-many universities and was known to be a scholar among others much like her. I knew this because she had said so to each one of us several times over – a mother is not just a mother; she can stop being a wife or mother when she wants to so long as she can come back to both; she has the choice of being a teacher or a preacher; she can beat us at will and she can pardon us any crime but she never will.

'Flowers, my dears, were humans in their previous birth who found salvation, all because of their goodness and faith in God,' explained Nani, as we grandchildren ate breakfast in practised synchrony, four of us trapped in the dining table circle.

Ma, who was proficient in the art of interruption, never let her finish. 'That is absolute rot and you know it! The children go to school where they study biology and physics and mathematics. Why do you waste your energy with old wives' tales? Science is the only god they will know.'

The brothers took that as a sign to get up from the table and march towards school. The same cane as the one I had encountered in the window-dahlia-cane episode had trained them to discern between a family squabble where one had to stay shut, and a conversation between adults where one still had to remain shut. I lingered on for as long as I could before someone noticed that I was not yet gone.

Nani wiped a tear with the corner of her sari. 'You talk like your father. The only difference is that he had the grace to put Science and God on different pedestals. Education is your undoing Sujatha. Education and pride.'

'My father gave me education. The pride is from you Ma. How can you not see it?'

The old spirit was not one to be badgered, 'If that is true, I have not been a good mother to you... and you, unfortunately, are repeating my mistakes with your children.'

'Oh, why won't you wear your dentures? Why did we get them made if you have to chew with your gums. It is revolting!'

'What do my dentures have to do with your children? I got them made because you would not leave me in peace otherwise. My gums are strong enough to crack nuts. Teeth are for the vain, not for those toothless from ageing!'

Ma pushed her specs up the bridge of her nose and refused to be baited into that argument. 'I don't wish to be late for classes. I will have lunch at the cafeteria.'

Nani often repeated how she came from the village to stay with my parents when my eldest brother was born to create chaos in their busy lifestyles. She fed, burped and put the infant to sleep while they scampered to their jobs in relief. With the second, third and fourth child coming in gap of a year each, the old lady stayed on reluctantly. She explained it to me in one word – 'circumstances' – a complicated concept to me then although I would have hugged her to my bosom from camaraderie now. Nani died for no reason, neither illness nor accident, but in her sleep, smiling like I had never known her to smile.

Education is a mirage and gives an illusion of wisdom. Our grandmother took her unqualified wisdom with her as quietly as possible. I can't even say that I missed her, so young and turbulent was I. Only Maria visibly seemed to resent the death, but that was because her million chores had expanded to include watering the garden. A few months after Nani's death, I saw the last of the yellow flowers outside my father's study. Soon the plants began to wilt, subdued into a drab existence by tall weeds.

Ma did her best to keep that part of a dead woman going. She paid a limping gardener every week to uproot all the plants and create a tender green lawn, the sort that came on the covers of glossy books or had been written about in poetic spirit by writers in distant countries. The gardener soon became a constant sorrow for her – temperamental, irregular and shirking work – but when he did turn up, she was grateful. Maria seemed to share that feeling, bringing the gardener as many glasses of water as he asked for and giggling from the kitchen window even when she knew him to be ugly and uncouth, not good enough even for idle distraction. She was an enticing girl who could not wait to burst into womanhood. Tall and dusky, her bouncy hair pulled up in a ponytail, Maria did all she could for us. The boys treated her in the manner they had seen my father do – curtly and with disinterest – and so she was particularly fond of me. I was quite content to provide the adulation and stayed close to her. Maria smelt like freshly cut grass, sometimes with a hint of lemon and sometimes the faintest camphor.

The flowers returned, more bountiful than Nani could have imagined. They burst out of scaly earth and swung in the air with giddying gaiety. Every breath we took became sweet and heavy with pollen. No two flowers appeared alike even if they hung to the same branch, every streak, every tinge blending into and over one another, till swirling around us were colours that all the books we read did not help us name. The gardener must have done something right.

Then, one day, Maria left us with heavy unhappy steps. The boy at the milk booth hung from the ceiling and the gardener never came by our house ever again. I wonder what Nani would have said to all that. Being the youngest and credited with the least intelligence, I was often allowed the privilege of being a fixture in the study when my parents had conversations that shuttled only between them and had nothing to do with us.

It was an overcast day and Ma kept flitting over to the window to decide whether the washing needed to be gathered and brought inside. She was saying, 'I can't remember the last time we had such heavy rains in Delhi...'

'Uh' was our father's ambiguous grunt which meant 'yes', 'no' and 'can't say' all at the same time.

'The clothes never seem to get dry...I was hoping that today would be different...maybe I should have them brought in ...surely it will rain again...*Maria! The clothes...*'

'Is she still here? I thought you said she would be gone.'

Ma pulled me off from the window where I was in danger of repeating my feat of being wedged and plonked me unceremoniously on the table. Pa dragged a paper from below my pants wanting – too late – to prevent the fresh ink from smudging. He looked at it carefully. There was some damage that would have to be ignored. He sighed and looked up at his wife as if he had just spied a stranger breaking into his lair, 'What do you want? I have...'

'...the thesis to complete,' she helped him complete the sentence, 'and we all know that...but what about Maria?'

'What about her? You said her father wanted to take her away.'

'I feel terrible. I explained the situation to him and he just stared at me as if we had failed in our duty towards him and

Maria. But she is a grown up girl… and I always took good care of her. We treated her right, didn't we Ratan? She always ate the same food as us. I bought her new clothes for both Diwali and Christmas. Now she won't even talk to me straight. I ask her a simple question and she turns to the wall to sniffle!'

The wind rattled the windows and so did the overweight raindrops that followed. Our clothes continued to flutter outside. I could see the pink polka dotted frock that my aunt had bought for me from her only trip to foreign shores. It was a good five sizes larger even when I pushed up every bit of spine which meant there was no danger of outgrowing the dress. Instead, I faced the constant pressure of having to grow into its gaping space. The last time I wore it on some silly social event, the hem of the dress hanging long, it got so dirty that Ma had it washed twice. Its imported grandeur was now reduced to looking limp and ugly beside Pa's snobbish white clothes as they slowly turned from damp to wet in the falling rain.

Ma shut the window and opened a door to yell at Maria again. *The clothes!* This time, there was a faint reply. I wished fervently the rain would drown my frock and Maria would forget to mention its loss. But that was too much wishing for any day to accomplish.

During this little distraction Pa, recovering his pen and wits, had returned to staring at the face of the table. Ma set me down on the floor and nudged me towards the door but I hung around to hear the rest.

'Ratan, how will I manage without her? She knows the household best and has been with the children almost all their lives. Let her stay here. What is one more mouth among all of us?'

'Her father knows what is best for her.'

'Who do you think it is?'

'Uh?' he was already turning a page.

'The father...'

'Hers?'

'Of the child that will be hers!' my mother was exasperated and I could sense the conversation fast winding up.

'Uh...' My father sounded very certain to my ears but just as swiftly must have forgotten who Maria was for I did not hear them talk of her again.

All the other children I knew went on summer vacations while we were made to take extra tuition to be sure we had a head start to the next academic year. All those other children had grandparents who lived in the countryside and doted on them with home grown fruits. We had only one grandmother in the name of relations and she did not care if we ate the plaster off the walls. She said – like all other animals, the young of a human know instinctively how to survive. She stayed with us mostly because there was nowhere else to go to. An ancestral house by the river ghats had been claimed by a distant cousin of her husband, who was lucky to have a briefcase full of crumpled legal papers. Those other children – the ones who enjoyed fruit orchards and vacations – were busy delighting in breaking rules while we patiently listened to our parents' debate on discipline. Thus we remained in that house within the sprawling university campus, parents with four children, a grandmother minus dentures and a blooming girl in floral clothes, year after year, faithfully observing the whimsical seasons that rushed by outside our walls.

6

I AM NOT TOO ENTHUSIASTIC ABOUT THIS HOUSE I HAPPEN to be cooped in; neither have I sought it out nor have the bricks come looking for me – two very important criteria in my esteem of memorable associations.

'I know you are awake. Stop pretending!'

I hear her voice but act otherwise. The night had wound long with thoughts and dreams playing cruel pranks on each other, exchanging identities, trying to merge and then scattering in opposite directions. Some of them, the ones too weak to escape, still cling to my eyelids, weighing them down in defiance of any resistance I might offer. I am content to surrender but the voice of the Great Sister is not one to be ignored easily. It has long dug its tentacles into the walls of the Big House, ringing without obstruction at anyone who desires to breathe and as one who is still a member of that needy group, I decide to groan a feeble protest – 'Morning?'

'*Noon!*' she shouts back, 'Your Highness, kindly say "noon"! Two meals in a row are all I can allow you to skip. What was wrong with dinner last night? And the breakfast tray comes back untouched too. Why are the rich starving?'

'Another noon...' I sigh to erode a little of the sarcasm from her voice that continues to bounce in weak echoes around the bed.

'You certainly don't have to take my word for it,' she says, denouncing subtle hints and equally willing to back up anything she might have said. 'Open your eyes! See for yourself! Why you would want to waste your brothers' money is beyond me...not to mention trying to imagine your own time, your own sun — *Look out of the window!*'

'The same...' a verdict in the lowest decibels. My eyes are swollen slits.

'Ah! Sure! The very same!' the tirade continues. 'A sun in the sky and a headache between my eyes. Everything always stays the same in this wretched place!'

The Great Sister does have a way of making words feel ashamed of themselves. It perhaps comes from being the most experienced hand in the building. She is never asked for explanations nor does she care to listen to anyone who might dare speak up. The only thing that shines about her is the oil in her hair which, so goes the legend, is replenished even before it is washed off. I presume that when she looks into the mirror, a fleshy face crowned by glistening strands pulled back into a dark bun, she probably sees a halo. There is contempt in her eyes for us, the weirdoes who have been vomited in here by the world — a world to which she walks back with her jaded leather purse every evening — just as for the other mortals who have had to suffer us. How exactly the Great Sister scorns herself, I am unable to say. But if there was a way to do so, I am certain she is well informed and practises it thoroughly every minute of her spare time.

The brothers said the Big House had been 'highly recommended'; the authorities here in their spotless clothes are the only happy faces to endorse theirs; meanwhile I end up with the dubious distinction of having the Great Sister visit me twice on her rounds. She always marches into my room to yank the sheets from where they are comfortably bunched around the neck right down to the ankles, regardless of my clattering teeth. On days when it is a trifle warm, the blanket in a lump under my feet catches her attention and is promptly dragged up to smother my face. Not once am I asked about my preferences.

The double rounds have sealed my fate. It is commonly perceived and taken for granted that I am dangerous in some inexplicable manner. It does not help that I am here only to 'rest those nerves' and on hardly any medication, something everyone knows and presumes to imply one of two things — either the wise ones in charge are unable to make up their minds on what ails me or have simply given up hope of any recovery. Most people must believe the latter for they look at me with the saddest expression.

During the initial row of weeks, I would interpret their scrutiny as a critique of my attire and instantly straighten the gown by its floppy sides. The costume, horrid to say the least, is the dregs of all that is happening in my life. There have been times when I have tried to lighten its solemnity with a few ribbons, even fluorescent buttons that the twins donated. The Great Sister rips off the decorations each time without a word. Since then my efforts have been concentrated on keeping those little holes she leaves behind from growing in size. And just to draw her attention to my troublesome situation, I have flatly turned away from starched new replacements and insist on wearing what I have. With new clothes and rosy cheeks that never miss meals, suffering can hardly expect to be itself. I would have more to say on the topic of the gown but the fear of my thoughts being heard by the competent woman keeps me reined in.

'What are you gibbering under your breath?' she growls and there being enough signs of a rejoinder, I wait politely, 'And why are you sitting there with your eyes shut?'

O, have the slits shut themselves? I am too sleepy to care. A dull resentment is beginning to grow inside me. The afternoon sun with its eagerness to scale heights is turning into a jagged piece of broken glass. Slicing into the shy light that permeates from its breast, it tosses the shreds in the air and scatters them into countless sparkles of brilliance. It is a day intent upon dazzling. Beyond challenge.

The Great Sister is rummaging at the far end of the room and I am glad to indulge in a silence that needs no justifying. She has made a regular habit of peering at every bare nook of the closet's wooden heart. I know what will emerge from the exercise – another version of the gown I am wearing. It will be draped over a chair till I have bathed and immediately slipped back in costume, as if my identity would loom into something fearsome without it.

Now I know it is tempting to sit in judgement and label me an idiot. I can tell you, it has been done before. But as I look at it – we are all equally blind, deaf and lame people trapped in a big bubble filled with innumerable smaller floating bubbles, watery circles that will dash each other to non-existence.

Sometimes though, one bubble will attach itself to another and both will survive the encounter. They will travel either as one entity or as a beautiful link in a tableau of light. Perhaps as mine does now with yours.

7

THOSE WERE HARD TIMES, NOT IN AN OLIVER TWISTY SORT of way but certainly dreary. I was the odd one, being told so a thousand times each day and not necessarily in words. Ma's cane visited my skin often but scant respect for corporal punishment kept my head above the waters. I defied her and never cared about being apologetic or being reformed.

Even in my most generous moments it is hard to say something charitable about schools and my choice of words would range between 'ridiculous' and 'redundant'. However, since my parents preferred death to private schools, we were sentenced to spend ten years each, forty years collectively, in a red-brick government school in the company of those who could afford no better and those stuck with equally mulish parents. I have to be fair and give this school credit for being free from any pretence of making sophisticated products out of us: we had to clear each grade with good marks, not miss school often enough to get noticed and never testify against any student no matter what the crime unless we wished to be the next victims. I don't think any school elsewhere would have been less meaningless.

The thing to be recorded as detached observation at this stage is that while the brothers thrived under the education system, I completely wilted. Nothing ever made sense to me: not the need to turn up at an absurdly early hour each day; not the stupid routine with the stupid tie that had to be done with a particular knot if one did not fancy being detained after the morning assembly; not the whole obsession with facts, numbers and marks; not the insistence on making a child work the whole day at books and expect them to do more at home in the evenings. The person who possibly thought of that last one deserved a romantic encounter with the Great Sister. They would no doubt copulate out of a sense of duty to nature and make flawless human beings.

I was far from flawless. I was a disgrace. Worse, I had to sit in the front row right below the nose of the teacher, owing to a special request by Ma. She had seen all the signs of a happy back-bencher in me even while changing my diapers and, no different from Prince Siddhartha's father, sought to undo the prophesy. I could have told her she was wasting her time but she was a stout believer that parents talked while children listened so I submitted to the shame and sat in that detested first row. The fact that I was taller than most others in class was not taken into account. The kids who struggled for a view of the blackboard behind me often boxed my head into slouching. It made the whole school experience particularly painful, and not just in a manner of speaking.

I solved that situation soon enough. There were plenty of fellow inmates who agreed with my views on education and would rather kiss a comic book instead of a theorem. A few discreet shuffling of seats later, I sat tall again and the comic readers crouched behind me. Everybody's problem solved except mine.

I still had to pay attention, avoid falling asleep and constantly nod false comprehension when the teacher took a breather between sentences. It was beginning to drive me crazy. I coped with occasional absences from the classroom. First I pretended it was an accident: the visit to the toilet took longer than anticipated and the next teacher being already in the class, I did not want to disturb the course of wisdom. Sometimes it was a farce – I was feeling faint and had to rest under a tree in the playground, it being an hour before I could walk again. I soon got brazen – meet me at the ice cream cart at lunch hour since I may or may not come for the biology class in the afternoon. Then there came whole days when I would leave for school with satchel and lunch box but not be subjected to a single word of knowledge. There was a quiet little corner in the school park where the trees tangled their branches with overgrown thickets. It was also the time I discovered those devastatingly nerve-wracking murder mysteries. Hercule Poirot and Perry Mason needed me. I could visualise the rest of my life trotting by in relative ease and anonymity beneath the bushes in the company of complicated criminal minds.

As it turned out, it did not take much sleuthing talents to discover that the tall girl in the front bench was missing.

8

THE FINGERS DRUM ON THE PLAIN FLAT SKY. FIRST LANGUIDLY, a frail struggling heart-beat. Then with force and angry assertion, deep booming sounds. It is the moment of birth.

Her footsteps and the rising rhythm of her anklets challenge the black space beyond. The tumbling night shivers. Primeval. A vastness beyond explanation or comprehension. Primordial. She is named Aditi.

The fingers dare move again. This time gently tracing an unseen line across the sky. Tracing, till it cuts space out of emptiness and becomes a horizon of the mildest light. In that womb of tranquillity, the gods themselves beg to be born. Aditi becomes their mother.

She, the custodian of light, is also the sister of darkness. She is infinity during the creation of life. Unbound. Daughter of Dakshaprajapati, wife of sage Kashyapa, Aditi hums eternal lullabies to her powerful sons.

9

FROM THE INSIDE EVERY LIFE IS A FAILURE.

I did not think that up. A depressed man called George Orwell did. To agree would mean to write away all of creation – life, death, and the chaos in between – even the ceremonial funerals that follow stark death, amusing the soul with one last grand lie. Do we really take all this trouble for something confirmed to be a failure?

'Even a moron would learn these simple additions if he spent eight hours every day in school.' Pa rapped the cane on the edge of the table, always the table but never at us. The fear of the thrashing, not the actual punishment, is discipline – he would tell visitors while all of us stood in a row by the window, our palms folded towards our bodies, our knees aligned with each other, waiting to be given permission to speak, to leave or just stay in ease. Ma in her starched saris would nod. She believed her husband to be an idealist who needed the security of his impractical beliefs. There is a different conviction she secretly gave all credit to. Good parenting is a good flogging – was her theory. Add to that – what works fine on donkeys, works on children too. Unfortunately for us, Ma was always the one acting on wise adages while her husband merely gave long winding lectures.

'What are you, son?' our father's cane patiently tapped the table again.

'A moron,' the eldest said without hesitation. We knew most conversations by rote. Backwards and forwards: our lines and everybody else's.

'You're worse than a moron. My roof is a place of learning. If I see these marks repeated in your half yearly exams, you will need to find a new place to stay. Where will you go?' he sighed as if it were a real consideration. For my brothers, it truly was. Like I said, there was no other place we knew of and banishment was unthinkable.

'I don't know,' the young voice was beginning to show possibilities of caving in. His results were not that bad but they were not the best among his peers as was naturally expected of children belonging to scholarly parents.

'Back to Neelimpath,' a greater silence followed Pa's ominous words, 'to be a cowherd like your ancestors.' It was a place we had heard plenty about but never visited. We were not welcome there.

Do girls become cowherds too? — I thought and also — Where did that man smoking a cigarette outside our house come from?

'Do you know how much grazing a cow does in a day? How many miles she walks? Do you know, son, how hard the skin of a buffalo is when you scrub it clean at the village stream?'

'Very far...very hard...'

Ma got up and walked out of the room. This was familiar and painful territory for her. The man was nothing if not repetitive. She had met him when they were new and promising young citizens of a new and promising young country, students and intellectuals, socialists and visionaries; theirs was assured to be a flawless union, a step to the utopian future. But living as they were in a social blur where a tag on the blood meant everything, he was a cowherd from a far off impoverished tribal land and she the only daughter of a learned priest who had lit up the ghats of the Ganga with his wisdom. It dawned on us early in life that there was more to Nani cursing the education we were tethered to. Without it, Ma would have been a pious brahmin's wife submitting to rituals, festivals and prayers. Pa, having been a miserable failure at animal husbandry, would have most certainly mortgaged his land for a song and lost all his dignity over local politics. They were changing their destiny. They were creating ours.

Ma's father, the wise man who said the soul's only identity is its goodness, choked on the emptiness of his preaching and died long before his daughter arranged her own nuptials. The cowherds fared a little better living somewhere in the dusty countryside. A family astrologer, blind in one eye and deaf in both ears, spat into my mother's horoscope, 'Her feet are dipped in blood. Keep her away from your family,' he told them but did not elaborate. The cowherds – only by caste, my father later told me, not really the rustic naked boys tending cows as seen in the movies and imagined by us – who were rich landlords, took the opportunity to show that they could scorn the high castes too. Our father soon found himself cut off from filial nourishment. So we never meet the relatives, neither his nor hers, excepting the flower-loving grandmother who died and the aunt who bought me the oversized dress.

Ma said I was that curse – every inch of me stamped with primitiveness, a girl cowherd without a herd. The boys, looking like peas in a pod were no doubt gifted with her fair daintiness. I thought it was more exciting being the curse and often said so, but never in her hearing.

10

I SAT WITH THE SCHOOL PEON ON THE BENCH OUTSIDE THE principal's office. He was a grey and bitter man: none of your kind janitors from the charming residential school adventure books. He abhorred children – his own and others. I am convinced that if he had been the ruler of some regressive clan, he would yoke the young to ploughs and make bonfires of books. The children of the school, drawn by their instinctive knowledge of his disdain for them, directed all their pranks and ire in that very direction, and with uncanny precision covered up all evidence so that the principal who heard the peon's many complaints was beginning to think him delusory. The man was often heard muttering that he would rather be a jailer than a school peon. Yet, such was his fate, poverty and misfortune that he sat beside me on the bench that day when my absconding from class was finally cracked down upon.

'I hate school,' I told him sagely.

'I hate it too,' he growled.

'Did you go to school when you were young?'

He dug into a little tobacco pouch with extreme care, as though it was his life, and ground the contents into his left palm with the right thumb. A piece of betelnut bounced off onto the dirty floor. I bent down and picked it up for him. He popped it in his mouth before it could escape again and did not care to look grateful for my effort.

'No, I did not go to school,' he said and with a dramatic pause, 'I thank Lord Narayana for that. I have learnt everything worth learning from the school of life. But mind you, all my boys went to schools that had proper benches. That is probably why they have abandoned their old parents to live as the wives tell them to.'

'Because they went to school?' I wondered, not minding the silence he glowered back. I was amazed and could not wait to tell Ma of this man's analysis of schooling which ought to put an end to claims of the brothers being the hope for the future and all that.

The principal pressed the buzzer just then. The peon swiftly threw the tobacco in his mouth and nudged me to stand up. I paused long enough to see one of my brothers staggering at the far end of the corridor. The rest of his class was trooping out in a line. He had broken away and did not look pleased at all to see me there, not out of concern for me but rather burdened with the duty that now lay on his shoulders of having to report what he saw because suppressing facts was no possibility. My father had knocked down too much morality down our throats for that. I waved cheerfully at him and followed the grouchy peon in.

'Why?' groaned the principal with his characteristic nervousness as he swivelled his chair left-right-left-right. 'Why are you so different from your brothers? And with parents so learned and cultured like yours...' Briefly, I thought he was trying to blame my parents for being that way and just as briefly I rejoiced. But then I saw his eyes express a very common doubt in the populace: perhaps I had been adopted or even mixed up in the hospital nursery, so little affiliation did I show with the rest of the family.

'I was meant to be a boy,' I told him cordially.

The explanation to this muddle will have to wait a little longer for just then I was keen to know what he had to say. A weak man by constitution and weaker by the demands of his job, he looked at the frowning peon who did not blink in deference.

Suddenly I saw that they were the ones who had been mixed up! The educated man in the chair had all the qualities required to sit diligently and humbly on a wooden bench in the corridor, responding to nothing but a little buzzer on the wall. And the angry man beside me, uneducated and liberated, put in charge of the school would have flogged sense into every child daring to be a deviant. There is no justice in the world, is there?

'During my days in the teachers' college, we believed...' the man condemned to his suit started the usual sermon. I heard a snort of contempt from the peon as he shuffled out of the door. In his disgusted mind (as also in mine) we already knew that I would soon be leaving the room with barely any retribution. It made me cheerful enough to listen to the prattle of a soggy mind now saying, '...I always argued that the best way to discipline a child was to free it from the fear of the cane...'

O yes, the cane again! I thought of the two that already made their presence felt in my childhood – the rough bough of a tree propped behind Ma's kitchen door that had often scarred my skin and the polished bamboo placed strategically on Pa's table to threaten but never put to use. Now talking to me was a man with an imaginary cane. I felt sorry for all of them – people and canes.

'I'm sorry,' I decided to cut a long process short.

'Sorry? Really? Will you attend your classes regularly?'

'No,' I told him honestly, having been assured that no physical pain was involved.

'So, what do you suggest we do?' He put his elbows on the table and leaned forward, his chair suddenly turning silent.

I knew I was not expected to answer. In any eventuality, I was trapped in the mind of a brother who at that very moment was sure to be composing his report on my battle with higher authorities. Ma would be here at the crack of the next day's dawn.

'I think I should have a word with your parents,' he said and pressed a little switch, not because he wanted to see the scornful man who would come in with all his hatred for both of us but because he wanted to assert some dominance, tell me that the meeting was no longer open to my opinions.

'Will you inform your parents or should I write a note?' he debated aloud.

'My brother will do that,' I assured him. 'He knows I am here.'

'Fine, I will have a word with one of your brothers,' he said, not gullible enough to take my word, 'but at this very moment will you go to class? Please?'

'Sure,' I shrugged and sauntered past the tobacco-scented peon who waited for the pale man in the noisy chair to think of something for him to do.

I headed straight for the school gate. The guard on duty did not blink as I waved farewell at him. If questioned, he would faithfully report my time of departure, but not being expressly ordered to detain anybody walking out as confidently as I did, he did not bother. I never returned to the school, not even for my books which had been forgotten somewhere and efficiently retrieved by one of the brothers.

That day I must have wandered the whole city, with no particular destination or mission, looking at this and sometimes at that, till by some coincidence I ended up in the same lane as my house with its lit windows. I walked in to interrupt a frantic hunt being chalked out to locate me. The kitchen cane came down hard on me that night. I cried without shame or restraint till the neighbours yelled out to Ma to stop. Luckily for me, they needed to sleep.

Soon after, it was the turn of the principal. Ma shouted at him for not taking proper action against an errant student. Pa said the least he could do was make sure I stayed within school premises. The peon of course was heard telling them without being asked that I should be married off instantly to someone they hated. He was ignored but not the principal who was browbeaten on his creaky chair till he turned yellow and sniffed into a yellowier hanky. When he finally spoke up, it was to bemoan that he only cared for teaching algebra because it was something the children either understood or didn't, easy for the first lot and not a great loss for the second but that was until some bureaucratic rule about seniority gave him this horrid punishment of a job. After my parents left, my brothers told me later, the algebra-man shut himself up in the room for an hour and emerged only late in the night when his face was as dark as the walls of his school.

11

HE STOOD AT THE CROSSROADS. EACH TIME THE CURTAINS parted a little, either from a swift casual swing of my arm or the teasing wind, I saw him there, exactly like the previous glimpse, almost a cardboard cut-out pasted on the night. Yet he was alive, if only in the movement of the cigarette that alternated between fingers and lip, with such precise rhythm that it could only be called mechanical. He was standing alone, in no hurry to leave or to finish his smoke, right there at the crossroad in front of our house.

A few shadows were moving apart from the shivering trees, all human shadows: students on their way to drinking sessions for which they had pooled their meagre resources; the more industrious ones walking for health; those crowded around a run-down takeaway van called 'The Golden Dragon' to eat oily noodles. Our home was only one of the many monotonous structures in the university campus. Pa and Ma had studied here, met here, found jobs here and continued to live here, impatiently goading the four of us to grow up. And grow we did. Even if someone told me of the existence of other places, I was only capable of conjuring up images of similar spartan buildings, straight tidy tarred roads with bright white paint markings and shrubs and trees perfectly aligned with each other. All I was willing to believe at that age was what I saw.

I saw a man smoking in the dark.

It is difficult to elaborate on why the most inane of things decide to become important to us but I simply had to know that man and the real reason he stood there outside our house. Why did he not hop into the bus as it came along, brightly lit, rattling and empty? Why did the darkness of the hour or the heaviness of the long hand of the clock not frighten him as it did me? Why did he just stand there, in his overcoat, smoking?

'Do you know how much grazing a cow does in a day? How many miles she walks? Do you know, son, how hard the skin of a buffalo is when you scrub it clean at the village stream?' my father was asking.

'Very far…very hard…'

Ma got up and walked out of the room. The man was nothing if not repetitive. Maria came in with four tall glasses of hot milk. Pa tumbled wearily into his chair, the cane rolling out of his hands and under the chair.

'Where is your book Aditi?' he suddenly remembered and looked straight at me. I ducked behind one of the brothers and they all stepped aside to ruthlessly make sure I get my due but the cane was nowhere in sight and neither was Ma.

'I…I don't have it.'

'Who does then?' His hands had already picked up one of the ageing maps off the shelf to look at absentmindedly. I knew I had a chance if I could take it.

'It fell out of the window…a little while ago…' I said. My brothers gasped. I invented excuses while they calmly went along with the rules.

'Go and fetch it then,' he mumbled, already forgetting that he had children. Even when we could not spell our names or memorise the house number, we all knew that he was chasing history, something about some lost civilisation that did not get its due recognition from folks. For years I thought the whole world knew of his academic worries, so vocal was he about some great revelation that would change the course of human destiny if unravelled. He had continued to moan about conjectures and convictions and hypothesis till his death and the civilisation was never found.

In the meanwhile, I had declared my homework to be in the garden when I had not even started on it. I was out in a flash, escaping the dusty gloom of the study, brushing against Maria's skirt and cajoling her to accompany me to the crossroad to meet the smoking man.

He was still there. The jauntily cocked hat turning greyer as we walked closer to him. Maria was a little nervous, not for fear of the man – she had learnt the ways a woman could make a man quiver in front of her, even strangers – but more for being out of Ma's earshot. We stopped at a safe distance. Maria held my hand firmly. She too feared my reputation for unpredictability. We probably stood there a minute in silence. Nothing changed. The security of the house was just a few yards behind us if anything untoward were to happen.

The man suddenly heaved in his overcoat. Maria almost made a dash back to the house but this time, I was the one who had taken grip of her hand. She stayed.

'Who are you?' I asked bravely.

'And who are you?'

'Aditi.'

'Me, a shadow,' came the reply like an echo. The voice was gentle and controlled and immediately soothed Maria, who presumed like everyone else, that perverts and kidnappers sounded like uncouth growling monsters. She stopped trying to pull me backwards and took a small step ahead. This could be amusing and her healthy appetite for life made it hard to resist romance even in its vaguest form.

'Why are you standing here?' I persisted.

'I have nowhere to go,' he said, and took a deep drag through his fingers but the stump had doused itself out. He threw it flippantly into the soil, bending his head so low he was barely a human form anymore and could have been mistaken for the post-box from the other side of the road.

'Do you stay here? ...in the university?' I asked.

'No, but you do and I think your mother is calling you,' he said and Maria gasped. In her anxiety and terror of Ma she pulled away from me and started hurrying back home. I know she expected me to return with her but I did not. She would suffer a great deal for that defiance of mine.

Ten minutes after that, I was safely back home. There were no physical injuries and only the lace on the front of my dress was slightly torn. The police, the neighbours and everyone who knew us chided Maria for her carelessness even as she wept to avoid looking at Ma's furious face. I did not step in to explain that it had all been my doing. Instead I was trying to recall and hold on to what preceded the shouting and the pulling and the sound of a man's boot running into the night.

The shadow had pulled me inside its overcoat, lifting me upon its chest in a great big squeeze. I was alert and sharply aware of everything that invaded my senses: the stubble on his face, the smell of dried sweat, the texture of his cotton shirt, the fumes of nicotine, the little plastic buttons my fingers closed over, the furry warmth of the coat, the darkness, the terrible darkness. Then he hugged me, his arms, wiry under the sleeves crossing themselves around my lungs, again and again, till I could barely breathe. All the shadows in the world came rushing into the folds of that coat and there was hardly any room for anyone – not for him, not for me.

kingdoms in twilight

12

THE TALE IS FALTERING IN THE TELLING FOR HUNGER HAS begun to calmly pace around me. I am not sure who might speak if I continue gutting memories – the hunger or me. A fly, mercifully, is here visiting. It gives me something to do while the sun scorches disdainfully over the roof. The fly is keen to dance, tottering on the ruffled bed sheets with its hairy toes – do flies have toes? I know ballet dancers do – frequently disappearing to alight on any other surface my drab room can offer, even taking the trouble to hum and play the music it jives to in its head. I silently applaud the persistence of the little fellow, possibly a little maddened from sundry adventures – silver foiled sweets, a rat dead for three days, a rich man's polished car, even a spoilt child's tear streaked face – all inspiring this fine act. The larger world outside has its ways of sending messages. Is this one addressed to me?

I must have been watching the fly for hours because the evening tea trolley is now rattling down the corridor. It does not stop at my door. Have I been inadvertently forgotten? People who speak little are often slotted close to furniture in the great scheme of existence. I am there on the list, probably a notch above a footstool but certainly trailing the fly now playing the perfect gentleman, settling on my folded arm but panting from the effort. I regret that I am unable to find any old scraps of food in the room to offer as a sign of my hospitality.

A gentle breeze sneaks in from the gap between the windowpane and the wooden frame to ruffle us ever so slightly. It occurs to me then that the window has been pulled shut. It also occurs to me that the fly perhaps does not choose to be with me. Is he as trapped as I am? I turn slowly to the window. He stays still from curiosity, shifting ever so little when I yank at the latch. The musty room protests as the fresh breath of the distant hills sweeps in. I gasp to acclimatise and looking down to my sleeve find the little visitor is gone. The desertion is poignant enough to crumble any lonely mortal heart. I have just spent an afternoon mistaking a prisoner's desperation to be the dance of a suitor.

The little noises from inside the Big House are migrating bit by bit to the garden. Most of the residents will be seen dotting the large sprawling greens during warm evenings such as this. The punishing obscurity of the walls blend a strong cocktail together with the mellifluous sounds of the open, one that never fails to hurry the blood through the veins. From my window, I can see the twins walking at a distance from the others over a small spread of cut grass that has been rotting and drying in different patches. They seem to be looking for something and at the same time nodding in tandem at birds flying back to their nests.

I hear a familiar sound. It is the bald man in the wheelchair who laughs loudly at every sun that sets in his sight. One of my brothers had dared to strike a conversation with him and was told, 'There is nothing, young-man-in-white-shirt, nothing in our universe as powerful as that big ball of fire…and yet, watch it fall!'. Before the brother could feign comprehension, the man had rolled in laughter, with the same mirth and intensity as he does every evening. Shaken, the brother had hurried back to my side. The-bald-man-who-laughs-at-the-sun was infinitely more eerie than the-sister-who-refuses-to-conform. I am not proud of the comparison but it does say something, doesn't it?

I am still at the window, bending out as far as I can to look at a patch of open sky, a dullest section of blue where one solitary chunk of curly cloud is floating towards the horizon to avoid being pierced by two persistent eagles. I watch the cloud uninterrupted till the last light of the day skims off the wings of the fading birds.

13

SO I CAN'T PAINT. MAYBE I CAN WRITE. I CAN CERTAINLY READ. From signboards to dictionaries, I have been taught for years never to disregard any alphabet in print that crosses paths with my eye. I send a little note to the authorities explaining that I need to access books from the town library under the presumption that there is indeed a town nearby with a library that bothers to stock books. The Great Sister is my emissary. She twists her lips in disgust but defers from adding any comments as my note slips into the gorge of her coat pockets.

The Big House has a collection of chairs in a beige coloured room that it calls a library. Lodged between the chairs, one stark wooden rack displays a host of benign magazines on gardening, cooking and the like. Occasionally we come by a bold-lettered cover that heralds a war, an ecological disaster or a triumphant politician, but those always retain their glossy looks from staying untouched. Understandably, in a sanatorium, reality is not miles away in a long-standing international dispute making that great breakthrough or a shuttle launching into space, but in this very hour and in learning to see it pass as gently as possible through the labyrinth of emptiness. Each second sits precariously on top of the previous second and balances the one that follows on its head; a tottering column of desolation, one that lacks even the minutest sense of purpose.

The books are delivered to my room and appear to have been randomly selected. Whoever was sent to collect them must have been more lost than caring to admit and picked a book each from differently labelled shelves. With a little effort, the beginning of which is just limited to turning pages without reading, I have begun to follow the words in bits and pieces. A sentence here, a page there, sometimes even a chapter somewhere – fiction, classics, poetry, all attach themselves to one another. I am reading almost all the time now.

I also read because the eyes demand work from me; of all the senses, they are particularly troublesome and fancy being occupied. The ears are safe in sealed walls; the tongue frozen into inaction by the sticky gruel they boil in the Big House; the nose has always seemed an unimportant appendage; and touch (I try hard to recollect what that is and fail) is indifferent; yes, vision is certainly what plagues me. Of course, it seems ridiculous that an artist, a writer, a poet has to regiment and feed a creative spirit. Does one have to read to be a writer? That question brings me back to where I began.

Animal Farm, Animal Farm, Never through me shalt thou come to harm!

'Come in! Come in!' he sobbed. 'Cathy, do come. Oh do – once more! Oh! My heart's darling! Hear me this time, Catherine! At last!'

I think, even, if I ever die, and they stick me in a cemetery, and I have a tombstone and all, it'll say 'Holden Caulfield' on it, and then what year I was born and what year I died, and then right under that it'll say 'Fuck you'.

STELL – LAHHHHH!

'Fish', he said, 'I love you and respect you very much but I will kill you dead before this day ends.'

'The horror! The horror!'

'She's a trifle fat about the middle because she's cooking up a little Zorba for me.'

For years people were not aware of the existence of a Municipality in Malgudi. The town was none the worse for it...

If this be error and upon me proved, I never writ, nor no man ever loved...

It was the same sun as the day of my mother's funeral

When all at once I saw a crowd, A host of golden daffodils.

It was the best of times, it was the worst of times.

Had I as many souls as there are stars…I believe that a revolution can begin from this one strand of straw…the owl and the pussy cat went to sea in a beautiful pea-green boat…

All happy families are alike.

Higgins: Say A, B, C, D.

Liza: But I'm sayin it. Aeyee, Be-yee, Ce-yee

It gives me a headache; all these words and phrases sticking to the retina like feathers dropped in a pot of glue. Tiresome. I turn a page here and a page there until nothing can induce me to venture towards another piece of paper. I lie exhausted. Every little movement in the room and outside among the trees magnifies into overlapping screeches that only my pounding head seems to hear. The moth flitting outside my window beats its wings as loud as the sails of a boat at storm; the droplets of water dripping from the leaky tap crash down the sink like a high tide on the rocks; even the ants travelling the line where the walls join, march like soldiers on cobbled pathways.

I pick up the book that is lying dormant and growing heavy on my chest. I stretch across to place it on the side table but it decides to fall on the floor. A sharp knock immediately jumps back at me from where the book is lying. The fat auntie who sleeps directly in the room below has made frequent scathing complaints of my dropping plates and objects with little regard for the sanity of those unfortunate enough to live on the ground level. Of late she has been finding ways to retaliate, mostly banging right back at me. I leave the book there, almost afraid to find a hole in the floor if I move it that would have me looking straight at her scowl.

I slip into my canvas shoes, wrap a shawl around my neck tightly like a muffler, its bulk barricading half my face, while pondering on the need to find someone to look at and to talk to. I need counsel. Around here, mature dependable companionship can only come from the young twins. They understand the unspoken and that it is the highest knowledge there is.

14

THE OVERHEAD SUN REFUSES TO CAST SHADOWS AND THE roof of the house has turned into an umbrella from its intrusive eyes. Afternoons stirred into lunch and spiked with sleep is a daily potent brew that easily clears the hallways. My destination is a large high-roofed corner at the far end of the house. Just before I close the door to my room, I remember the borrowed paint brushes and plunge right back into the untidy piles of books around my bed. Everything is overturned and then put back into its place. Untidiness has its own aesthetics. The paint brushes are laying quietly, a page marker in a book of indecipherable alien script that has sneaked in with the rest of the contingent. I hurry out.

The twins look up as if they have been expecting me, in one synchronised movement that makes it easy to forget that there are two of them. The blankness in their eyes is unwavering. Far in the distance someone coughs a lung dry; the reverberations vibrate in the air long after the voice turns silent. I nod apologetically to both the boys as they bend over a cross-eyed doll that is trapped between four hands. One of them calmly plucks the plastic head off its neck while the other settles down to colour the doll's pale off-white socks. Have I mentioned that watching these boys could merit as an occupation in itself?

Having been in the Big House longer than anyone else has planted plenty of gossip about the twins. Most agree on it being rather doubtful whether they know any place apart from this room and these windows that slice walls to overlook an unkempt garden, beyond which again rise another layer of solid brick wall, taller and graver. Much ambiguity swirls around the twins but never is their sensibility disputed. If you don't have a word to say – the Great Sister is known to say – you are either an idiot or the wisest of saints. I quote her with reverence being in the presence of little gods that wield paintbrushes instead of ugly golden bows.

Except for that brief instant when I had stepped in through the door, the twins have been busy with their many preoccupations. My comfort comes from being aware that their general attitude of disinterest applies to each other too. It is this plaintive intensity, doubled by there being two of them, that draws people around to cater to their unspoken needs. The only other things that say anything at all in the room are large drawings on the walls. Starting from an inch above the floor – made during the time when the twins first came to the room as toddlers – the sketches have evolved with the addition of many feet in height. Mostly abstracts, but for an occasional limp stick-man, the geometric shapes ooze bizarre psychedelic colours. I have known of learned visitors often brought in just to have a closer look at the art forms, voyeurs, who after an hour or so of breaking against hostile cryptic visualisation, probably returned to interpreting dreams.

I wonder if I ought to confide of my mishap with the art world. Probably not. The gut instinct – if it could be reasonably accepted that the gut has an instinct independent of the rest of us – says that in their quaint ways the little ones are in the know of that. At regular intervals they draw deep noisy breaths, once even sighing at my face.

I watch carefully as one twin doodles a long snake on the wall, standing erect on the tip of his hooked tail (the snake, not the twin) and looking out of the window with its modest hood. The wind that brushes by the panes seems to intimidate the reptile briefly but it continues to endure. I can now see a crucial flaw in my existence. If I am an artist – seed meant to be tree – art should come to me naturally. So far, it has not. I have the appetite for sublime joy when it is scattered before me. I can soak the silliest of verse into my heart. I have drawn the grandest of canvases in my mind. And yet I have nothing to show to the twins or the rest of the world. I have nothing but the vision of greatness. Nothingness as always is delightfully itself, but how far can I stretch it in a lifetime that bores me with its projected longevity?

I sit down on the floor and pull the brushes from my pocket and place it carefully in the centre of a tile on the floor. The twins look at it sympathetically but don't claim ownership. The brushes continue to suffer their ignominy.

'I think they are better off with you,' I say, still not comfortable with dubbing myself a failure.

The twins furiously dab paint on the wall. I feel ashamed. Shallow and insecure beings are the ones who have to layer and complicate themselves. Evolved ones are always simple. And so it is with them.

'Well, yes, it is not the fault of the bush. It did not ask to be painted. But these things should come naturally. What use is art if it needs so much effort and struggle?' I fumble.

The dried bristles, stiff with soluble colours and my bout of anger, spread out against the white of the floor like a brown splayed flower. One twin looks at the other and he wearily trots off to fetch a glass of water. The brushes are soon soaking in their bath, hog's hair now flowers closing their secrets into a bud. Speaking of which, where are these hogs and the people who pluck out their hair for art?

'Yes, I know it is obvious. The true nature of things never changes. Only forms do. Why question that which is free from answers?' I sigh in agreement. In the distance the clock chimes. I get up to leave.

The twins turn away from the brushes and me. On the wall closest to us, a half-coloured butterfly is demanding their attention. A butterfly, to me, is the one who has struck the perfect bargain with creation: beauty, constant admirers, flowers for company, sunlight for happiness, cool wind for a little melancholy and then a swift death after a breathless lifetime.

The twins gravitate a little towards each other and I am dismissed.

The house vibrates gently under my feet as I walk its corridors. My room is very distant and irretrievably lost in that cosmic loneliness. Have I just woken up from a long nightmare to find myself in some fiendish future where all the people have migrated to a more habitable planet, forgetting me behind in a house with its contemptuous ceilings and cynical floors?

A bulky shape hops out just then from an elevator painted the same colour as the wall. I whine instinctively. The Great Sister looks me in the face, equally startled.

'And what do you think you are investigating? This place is not equipped to handle such unauthorised strolls, considering you are a menace even in your room,' she gives me a shrewd measuring look. 'You had better leave the twins alone.'

Trying to keep pace with her as she hurtles towards my room, I can feel the mental leash tug at my throat and have to run to keep from getting choked. 'Why are the twins here?' I ask huffing.

'Why are you here?'

'I don't know. But it is better here than where I came from,' I tell her honestly to which she snorts loudly.

'You're looking fine. I am sure you're eager to go home soon.'

'No' I assure her.

'No? Why no?' she is relentless.

'Why why?' I want to know.

'Why why what?'

'Why not no?'

'You are as sane as I am so don't try to convince me otherwise! Just stay away from the twins. They are coming along nicely…if only they would not scratch so much on the walls…they might just go back home to their parents.'

'My parents are dead.'

'And that is so much the nicer for them than having to see you here, wasting away like this.' She nudges me through the door to my room and closes it tight before I can retort. I head straight for the bed and tuck myself in. It is infinitely harder to quieten the mind. I continue to see those wonderful little works of art bursting out of the walls; much like having the Sistine Chapel or the Ajanta Caves in one's backyard; images saying things that I dare not begin to comprehend and I feel as rich as a sultan born in times of plenty.

15

IF THE THINNEST VEIL IS THROWN OVER MY HEAD, I'LL TAKE a deep breath to help it settle its weight; if I have a destiny trailing me for a lifetime, I'll surely wait for it to keep pace with me; if there is a God claiming authorship for my days, I'll possibly know to read that too; but the pressure of having to 'do' has numbed me to the core. Even before I really knew the parents who begot me or the brothers who had used the same womb before I could, I was told to hold up my head and prove myself worthy of the space I took in the world — to study hard, to be morally upright, to set goals that then needed achieving, to preserve my place in society by doing all whatever was generally thought agreeable and if possible, to be both ordinary and extraordinary at the same time. To begin with I complied. A little later I strayed. And then one day I simply rebelled. I wanted to be able to do things that were not anchored to any explanation nor had any end in sight.

I had opened the door to the darkness around, run out to the enticing stranger at the crossroads but having been there, got trapped in a memory, not knowing the route of return or the emergency exit. Perhaps that is the reason I am here in the Big House.

Now, having decided to write, there is perhaps nothing better than this to write about. Maybe in sharing a little of what I know and guessing my way though all that I do not, I will find my way out of these walls – not to leave but to simply know. Mostly, I end up with only one word to show for an entire day's work, a single word – and there is no need to pick up the dictionary, so common is this word – sitting pretty in a corner of a blank page. I am putting it there not because I can't do better but because it pleases me to do so. Who decides that pages have to be crammed with words? The single-word-days are frequent but never cease to amaze. I often get restless while lounging in bed at dawn – what word might await me today?

Sometimes I try to re-create whole episodes from the lives of people I have known in the past. Those sentences usually stagger confusedly to the centre of the page, inebriated and contorted; then I can't tell the character apart from the sentence.

And now I am beginning to notice odd things: the pen in my hands, its awkward shape, bloated in the centre and narrow on both ends, the way it presses against my skin to make small discoloured craters, the dull whiteness between lines that exist to ensure parallel sentences, how the page surrenders and gets indented when the pen forces itself, the sound – o that infernal sound! – of writing, those pages that cling to each other when I turn them or those that flutter without warning. When I do manage to fill a page, simply because the words quickly fall down in a row and then spill over into the next, I am so exhausted that I don't leave my bed for the next three days or so.

The brothers are supposed to check in on me this weekend. It is a grave sentence they bear with little grace. Three of them uneasy visiting and pitted against me who is content with all that comes my way – it is no contest. I fare better each time.

A hurried stooped figure walks in and turns on the lights in my room. The day must be beating a hastier retreat than usual. I am still twiddling with an adjective when the brothers reluctantly troop in. They spread around, staring at the wobbly piles of books stacked all around me, one heap ambitiously seeking the ceiling. I have taken some effort to scream my lungs out each time anyone thought of rearranging the room. There are books in every place possible, spilling over the table, crammed under the bed, some with folded ears so that I can catch up on incomplete sentences at inspired moments.

The whole sequence, of events and talk, has been performed in various seasons and so frequently that it has nothing new to offer. I sit back to endure. The brothers are saying the usual words and it must be borne in mind that we all mostly speak at the same time making the following order of speech quite arbitrary.

'How much longer do you want to continue like this?'

'All I wish to do is to think some things through.'

'And have you?'

'The process…'

'…the madness, we say! Why are you being so obstinate? This place is not for you.'

'You are being difficult. That is not what we mean and you know it!'

The familiar oiled head pops through the door for the regular tryst with my blanket but the bandwagon of brothers seem to repulse her. She bounces out of view. Darkness that had sprouted within the room now sneaks out from the open window behind my back to smudge itself into the sky. We sit in shared silence before they file out one by one, three faces, three names that have morphed effectively into one another in the last couple of years. Their expressions, clothes and postures blend till I hardly know one from the other.

16

ONE STIFF HOT EVENING, NOT TOO LONG AFTER THAT VISIT by the brothers, I am wheeled out of my room at nine after another highly forgettable dinner – wheeled, not because I am unable to walk but because I have seen so many printed words and so many unhappy brothers that I keep walking into walls without provocation. Two bruises later, the rusty iron chair with rustier wheels has been pulled out from below the staircase. Far from putting up a fight, I hum a merry tune during the creaky journey that takes me through the corridors and archways, some of which I am seeing today for the first time, new and unfamiliar burrows under the old relentless roof. In my mind, I can sense an unwinding spool of anticipation, more wayward than I have known for a long time now.

They wheel her in at ten in much the same way and switch the lights off immediately as if the sight of both of us together is simply unbearable. As far as I can tell, her two feet are intact too. All that remains when the door slams shut is the stuffiness of the room and the resplendent whiteness of her eyes. The new room is large and terribly bare, not a single book in sight, a décor I am beginning to like. With no place to hide and an hour or so of sitting upright in our respective beds, separated by three measured feet, she speaks the first words.

The strained voice approaches me like the hypnotic hissing of a glittery-eyed serpent. 'Did they bring you here for the same reason?'

'What reason?'

'Eating rice,' she says with finality and I imagine her clutching the edge of her cot.

'I wish I knew for sure. But it is certainly not on account of my diet,' my mind turns on the rice issue, 'In fact, I have often been given the option of feeding myself on the wealth of the brothers and live the life of a vulture. It is just not tempting enough,' I explain patiently.

'Hmmm…a vulture…' she ponders. 'I am the blacksmith's daughter.'

'It is very nice to get acquainted with you,' I say in my kindest voice but perhaps not kind enough for there are no more words from her side of the room.

It is a long night. My eyes close on account of their own weakness after an hour. Much later, when the night has locked its doors too tight for even starlight to sneak in, I wake briefly to find myself still sitting upright. So is the blacksmith's daughter. Sleep and consciousness tug at me from opposite ends. I can feel my muscles slip into an immeasurable emptiness, vaguely aware that my room-mate has picked herself up and glided out of the door as I am being pulled by a fatigue that has little sense of timing. I slide deeper into the blanket and curl up in happy surrender.

In the morning, my eyes open to confront a room larger than my own and know the night had not entirely been a dream. There is also a second cot near me, empty and immaculately made. Soon, at the striking of an invisible clock, the usual rush commences. Trolleys clatter up and down the corridor to the beat of worn out shoes. A young preoccupied face enters in a flurry of white to thrust me towards the bathroom where I ruffle my hair some more and saunter back into bed. The breakfast tray comes in and stays just long enough for me to grab a few bites; the lady with the fresh sheets; the man with the watering plant who growls a few words at the sole chrysanthemum perched on the window sill; the cleaning boys always in a hurry to leave; every visitor pretending to be the only one under the roof, replying to nothing, asking no questions; all cogs in the massive unseen wheel. I fidget with my gown wondering when the blacksmith's daughter will make her appearance.

She does return but only in the evening and leaning on the arm of one of the authorities, both faces serious enough to discourage queries. I watch cagily as she settles into bed and draws a sheet over her face. People have taken pains to invent so many redundant things, including boxes they can fill with images that talk incessantly. Why didn't someone have the ingenuity to create a machine that could effortlessly compress time and create more when required? Or even better, one which can sense the moment and mood of each day to generate little nuggets of phrases people can toss at each other in that tedious old game called conversation.

We are kindred spirits, the blacksmith's daughter and me. I know it in the way she moves to avoid disturbing the clutter of odd objects I strew around the floor for amusement; brushing her teeth and washing my toothbrush to show that I have done the same; exchanging the contents of our thrifty closets, I a little stretched in her clothes and she swimming in mine. However, it is mostly in the way she keeps pushing her plate of food wordlessly at me, pleading with her eyes to finish it for her, that I know her to be a friend. At certain times, it does disturb me to note her complete lack of appetite and manner of eating, no different than a bird with tonsillitis. But what of that you might say? I can't help wondering – they are giving her rice to eat here and yet, despite her self professed taste for it, she rarely swallows more than a morsel.

We partake of each other's silences. I have never known anything more blissful, never been in the company of another person who did not expect me to speak or feel compelled to drop a few civil sentences every now and then. She is content with herself the way I am with me. We sit on our beds, look out of the windows, take separate walks in the garden, eat while the spoons speak, crinkle our eyes at the same morning light, sleep long hours with minds shut in regard for the other's dreams. Visitors to the room, no matter what the hour, inquisitive to know whether we benefit from company, see us sit in beatific stillness and go away disconcerted — is this what was expected to happen? Something has to change and they knew it with their uncanny animal instincts. Two spheres of energies cannot be in the same room and remain unaltered by each other no matter how trivial the change. It was just not possible. We knew it too — the blacksmith's daughter smiling to herself frequently in unabated amusement especially when Time began to gather its skirt and run, the hours heaving as its random pleats. I am re-learning what I already understand: take away all soul-searching, even the identity of the self and what remains is a bottomless calm. We have said very little since those first few words. She is emptying herself. I watch and try to do the same.

Then arrives the storm. It is not entirely unexpected. The skies have been continuously shifting from an onslaught of heat rising off the earth. Some of the mountains try to block the clouds in protest till an intense violet gathers around the peaks. Everyone seems to talk of nothing else but the delightful overcast days that defy the summer. We both look out of the window often. An equally grave cloud is beginning to stalk the blacksmith's daughter's face as the calm slowly turns to brooding. This cannot be a good sign. As long as she was inactive within, I had been comfortable reciprocating. But here she is, the thoughts swinging around in her head, and I hear every little swish of its advance. It makes my head throb to an unnatural violent rhythm. If it rains soon we might endure, otherwise there is a chance that she might explode with her thoughts and I with mine.

<h1 style="text-align:center">17</h1>

IT IS A STATE OF WAKING SLUMBER, SO TORTUROUS THAT THE eyes glue shut, mind paces its darkest alleys, mouth denounces itself and the ears are assaulted by the shrieks of the dead. The storm descends with a vengeance. Furious winds battle long and hard to scatter the water drops before they dissolve into the hillsides. Listening to thunder is so commonplace that we don't even flinch when the walls rumble and windows regularly shatter in shame. The Big House almost spreads its wings to take off with the lightning but I fancy our weight pinning it down.

I am in bed, so immobile that I may just as well be dead. The flashes and howls from outside of little consequence to me, falls directly on the blacksmith's daughter. I watch her flip in her bed, a fish in a net looking at the sky for the first time. I wonder if anyone needs to be intimated, from this world or any other.

She breaks the long silence but as if it were a terrible mistake to do so. 'They will come for me soon,' she whispers.

'Splendid!' I say in good spirits.

Am I mistaking a complaint for anticipation? By the side of each of our beds is a switch with the picture of a calling bell to seek assistance. I firmly squash the image of the little bell from my mind.

She shakes her head and gets up to lock the door and the windows, twice undoing the latch and securing it again. I know I should feel concern, but in her gown – uglier than mine, for it has emerged from a wash with a forgotten red scarf with smudges of pink– and her tiny bare feet, she can easily be a puppy; an impish puppy turned ponderous after its first taste of being pelted with stones. She sits at the frontier of her bed, the very edge, where leaning forward would mean kissing the floor.

And she speaks, 'They…banished…me…the kingdom,' every word a distinct whimper of pain. I wonder if the storm is blowing some important words away from me but don't dare ask for a repeat knowing like everyone else about walls and ears. I open my mouth but not to spill sagely wisdom. Far from it. The logical response should be – What kingdom do you belong to? But I choose instead to be more relevant – Why? It seems a fair direction to probe for I imagine both of us belong to the same manic mob. What I call society, she probably thinks of as kingdom.

'For what?' I rephrase the thought as she turns anxiously and breathes heavily, the bed creaking soulfully under her.

'How can I trust you?' she asks.

'You can't.'

We sit still as the window panes tremble in the presence of another gigantic outburst from the mountains now completely hidden behind a curtain of dark swollen bags of vapour. The whole world is turning grey. No day, no night, just time that is thrashed clear of every sliver of light or colour. She waits. My conscience, which insists on a reclusive life, is waking – comfort her, it says. But how can I? – I grumble back – I will not rely on anyone, not even myself. Don't we tread over a large desert full of shimmering pools of water, most of them illusory? How is one to ever know for certain when one image of water will pulsate with ripples if dived into, while another is certain to vanish into air?

She speaks again, 'There was a time when I thought I was right and everyone was wrong. It was a thought that made me happy. But then, I learnt that everyone is always right. And if you are not part of that everyone, then you must be quiet. In a land where people eat shit, the rice-eater is the fool.'

Rather drastic, I think, but do not say so.

'One has to eat shit like the others or eat rice quietly and not tell a soul,' she continues to confide. 'If you make a different choice than the rest, never say it aloud like I did,' her voice turns softer and incredibly sad.

Before I can tell her that she is better off without this kingdom she pines for and that she is lucky to be in the Big House, even if the people here are no less quirky and oppressive, the blacksmith's daughter gets up to glide around the room, touching the walls lightly with her fingers.

'I am frightened,' she says and the little bell comes to mind again.

Shall I just bear the burden of this moment or simply let the bell do it? Undecided, I blurt out what I have been thinking all these days, 'Why do birds swim and fish fly? What we do is not what we are meant to do. And what we are meant to do...'

She turns calm but continues to walk along the walls so steadily that my neck turns on its own axis without effort. The steady sound of rain fills the room through the tightly fastened windows. The storm is lapsing into a soothing rhythm and she resumes, 'There were just too many of them. *A whole kingdom!*'

I shake my head at the emphasis, 'Did all of them do the very same things? Eat the very same...?'

'Yes,' she nods. 'It is not about conforming or rebelling. The life one is born into, doing the same things as our parents and growing up to be them all over again — that is about building pathways over existing ones. To not do so is to allow the grass to grow back on the road.'

I can figure this — the road is the road because people walk on it. We yoke our spirits with that of our ancestors in the hope that the road is not entirely lost to the grass likely to grow over it. And when we do hop off, wanting to tread the tall unruly foliage, we are starting where the previous walkers did, making another road and hoping there will be others who will walk behind us so that the grass does not wipe our toil away.

I am pleased with myself. However, my companion continues to move from one tale to another, not a single sentence alluding to her own experiences. The most exquisite but terrifying events and people walk the stairways of her memories; they swim in all dimensions, swell up in giant hallucinations, slither underneath the feet in unseen waves of torment. For some tales, I imagine she is walking down little tunnels of facts. My eyes blink in attention for a familiar acquaintance or two. However she is always pulling her story to greater heights, the unreal seducing her entirely, and gradually, me too.

I listen for hours and her voice begins to sound increasingly like my own.

Kingdoms sweep through the narratives, her own pushed aside for now; most of them far-flung, a few on different planets even; some sound credible, very near, very frightfully near. One of those worlds holds me in its thrall. I will always remember the warmth of its surface, the chill of its plunging depths, the pull of its sweeping breath.

18

ONCE THERE WAS, AND ONCE THERE WAS NOT, A KINGDOM ruled by the tongues. The unimaginative would perhaps describe it as a community where people had lost all control over their speech. Nobody remembered the day that first happened or the reason behind it: maybe they were too busy ridiculing and cursing each other. Somehow all the tongues in that land had cultivated minds of their own, like a fearsome cult, working like whips and thinking like tyrants, independent of the people whose mouths they were inevitably attached to.

Over the many years, those living in that kingdom came to see themselves as different from folks elsewhere. Or maybe the tongues took that decision. All trade was conducted within themselves. They chattered all the time, humiliating the hands that worked and goaded them into greater productivity, for talking did not fill the belly. In the markets they haggled and cursed ceaselessly, each wanting the best deal. The louder tongues usually prevailed, losing out only to the more vicious ones who compensated the volume of their voices with the merciless sarcasm in their slightest whispers. The only silent ones were the homicidal tongues that lashed out when they sought to kill. Everyone steered clear of those. They were the most unpredictable.

These powerful tongues were astute enough to realise that their race was best protected by sealing it against foolish and tame tongues elsewhere that were yet to establish supremacy over the human heads they rested in. All marriages were negotiated and limited to the kingdom. Any stray offer for an alliance that came from distant lands, mistaking their prosperity and abundance for goodness, was answered back with the choicest of insults. The tongues thought themselves to be very superior, the chosen ones who deserved God's land more than God himself, tongue-less that he was.

Marriages in the kingdom were bound to be strange. Those involving plenty of arguments survived the longest. The quieter ones were bound to end in bitter divorces: this according to annual surveys conducted by those tongues that wished to dedicate themselves to cultural preservation. With children, the figures were very ambiguous. Children with active tongues as well as those with slow ones were found to be equally difficult. The young learnt their tricks early. The more malicious a child, the more he was bound to be appreciated. Every now and then, a child managed to somehow escape the scalding effects of being under the reign of the tongues. As did the chieftain's only son. Born without the ability to either hear or speak, he was blessed with a fine chiselled face and soft curly hair that made a natural glowing crown. As for the calm and radiance on his face, that perhaps came from not having heard a single harsh word in his life. His tongue, having nothing to say, submitted to the natural rhythm of his head and inner spirit.

During one of his solitary ramblings across the countryside, for he had a nomadic side to him, the young man fell in love. A beautiful peasant girl with her herd of goats had drifted too close to the kingdom of the tongues. Her womanly heart could scarce resist the vibrant goodness on the young man's smiling face. Mesmerised, she let him hold her hand and kiss away the sweat from her sun-baked lips.

The young man had found his bride. All tongues joined force to try and dissuade him, but what might have melted any other mortal was wasted on the deaf boy. Hearing only the quickening of his own heartbeats, he remained adamant and began to pine away for the lovely girl. For many weeks, the boy turned his face from his family, his childhood friends, even his meals, till everyone was forced to reconsider their objections. The tongues finally relented, confident that they would be able to conquer an illiterate young woman even if she were born elsewhere, and impress on her the need to submit to vile speech.

The marriage was a pompous affair. The tongues spared nothing to show the world that they could be magnanimous too. At the same time they plotted to corrupt the untamed stranger who was yet so nauseatingly sweet. The bride had no regrets about marrying a man who neither heard her nor expressed his love in words. She was willing to cast her eyes shyly to the floor and submit to the desire in his young earnest eyes.

The tongues could barely wait for the wedding festivities to die. They attacked the bride, throwing undeserved insults, picking on her every move, wagging their malice on her every waking moment, hissing evil thoughts through the walls in the nights when she lay in the arms of a man who was unable to hear the offenders or her misery.

(The blacksmith's daughter took a breather to tell me what *she* thought of the tongues – there is no greater weapon than a human tongue; it twists any way it wants; no bone, no spine, both dangerous and loathsome; a venomous snake trapped inside a human body.)

The young bride nearly took flight. The sweetness of her father's home visited her dreams. She craved for kindness and would have paid for it, if she could, with food or sleep or even her life. There was, however, one force she knew of to defend herself against the tongues. Music. So one night, her heart heavy with the poison constantly injected into it, she recalled a few notes of a lullaby her mother used to sing. And as she cried for her parental hearth, the stray tunes briefly drowned the sound of the tongues. The brightness of the many dewy dawns when she had taken the goats to graze had found home in her voice as also the poignant star-lit nights of loneliness in a hostile land. She sang like the nightingales who had been frightened away from the kingdom by the din of quarrels.

That moment onwards, each time the tongues lashed out at her, the young girl took to singing. There having never been a singer before in their midst, the kingdom was wrought with confusion. What could they do against these new enticing sounds that rang out of the chieftain's house? Nothing they could say, and no matter how much they shouted it, could match the sheer charm and allurement of the girl's voice.

As the young bride sang, the birds returned to the land to join her with their own music. Alarmed, the people tried gagging her but now the birds sang louder instead. Countless insects, bees and small creatures of the grass woke from their stupor to hum in the chorus. Enchanted peacocks hesitantly checked the ground with their scrawny legs to tap out the beat. The whole composition soon reached such a crescendo that it drowned the sound of all tongues, and the heads – after many years of subordination – suddenly regained control of the senses.

The bewildered and vanquished tongues found themselves saying only what the heads were thinking, which being neither song nor filth, was mostly the mundane. And with that, peace descended on the land.

19

THERE IS A MOMENT IN EVERY DAWN AND DUSK, ONE fleeting moment, when the sky turns fluid and the sun appears to be undecided, when it is difficult to tell sunrise from sunset. One such moment comes along unannounced every now and then, lingers awhile, leaves both joy and pain behind. The blacksmith's daughter quietly ends her tale. The storm is beating a weary but triumphant retreat. The room turns colder. We slip under our blankets. I feel heavy in the head but light in my feet. A good yarn has that effect on me — hugging from the inside and crushing the bones till every breath needs accounting for. So while I don't know for sure about tales having ends, I do know they have arms, long heavy arms. I let myself be picked, twirled around and carried away into the haze.

Almost everyone lines up to participate in a vision that moves like a cyclone under my closed eyes. The Great Sister is ripping apart my grandmother's dahlias; Maria is ten years old and struggling up a hillside with a belly that bulges to her knees; the school peon is serving ice-cream in our kitchen to the brothers who are all grey and wrinkled; the dog is only half dog, the rest of him is fish; Ma is crying because she cannot find a knife to scrape the toast; the stranger in the coat has come to visit me without his clothes; and Nimmi is dead, killed by Nandita's switchblade.

I wake.

The breakfast odours cling to the damp house attaching itself to everything that moves. I prop myself on one elbow, wishing for a calendar for the first time in a long while, wanting to know what day of the week I have woken into, what month, what season.

The bed next to me is empty.

'She is gone,' they say, looking at me as though I have swallowed her up.

I miss her but would have been more disappointed if she had stayed to let daylight strip her of secrets that had been shared in the dark. The blacksmith's daughter does not return and I am moved back to my old room.

memories

20

LONG DARK PATTERNS OF THE NIGHT WERE LAYERED ACROSS the floor of the entire house. I stood in a pool of darkness between two rooms, not wanting to be noticed but the house called out for my attention. The gentle creaking of the many wooden almirahs as they gave way to the fatigue of the years, the scrambling of cockroaches that lived in perfect solitude in dusty bookshelves, the snoring of a tired brother after a long tiring day, the noises of a waking brother as he shuffled in the basement, the clicking of the refrigerator stabiliser that fought against fluctuating power and a wind that dared not say too much on that clear starlit night. I stood at the threshold and listened closely.

In the small porch, separated from the overgrown garden by tall grills instead of a brick wall, a brother slept with the dog. I stepped ahead and moonlight fell on my feet. The dog opened one eye lazily. I waved my hand at him and he shut the eye in disgust. He was possessive about his sleep and resented being talked to. I mean, most people talk to their dogs but in our house the dog was always planted thick in the middle of one-sided conversations. Everyone chatted with him. It was like an infectious disease that someone mistakenly got saddled with and then gave to the rest. In the beginning, he must have liked the attention — I remember him cocking his head to look about adoringly. Then, gradually, when it became clear to him that everyone just happened to talk when he was around, much the same way that people talked to themselves in the loneliness of the Big House, he folded his ears and turned away in disinterest, often taking refuge in alluring dreams, his limbs flaying wildly for an imaginary prance through a fantasy land.

Ma in her last years, certain that she was dying and having outlived her husband who had always been the more driven of the two, wanted to be sure about having a companion she could look at when it was her turn to go. The dog came home with her after a habitual evening walk and stayed on to take Pa's place.

'Who is that?' Amar had asked. He is the eldest son and often took the lead with questions.

'The dog,' she shrugged, and nobody bothered to name him after that. If he needed to be called, a sharp whistle worked better than words. Soon we called him whatever we fancied and the dog smartly figured that any name that did not belong to the rest of the family was his due.

Maybe it was Ma who started talking to him. Or maybe one of the brothers. It was certainly not me. For many months I watched as the dog was addressed to in matters of settling domestic bills, the happenings of the day, the local gossip, even the weather. His ears soon refused to rise at the magic words 'walk' or 'food' for it was inevitably lost in the rest of the banter. I have known of times when more than one person would talk to him instead of each other.

'Something went wrong somewhere with these children,' Ma would grumble, 'I cannot even remember when but I have no hope for any of them now.'

'And such angelic children they were…well, the boys surely were,' added her visiting sister during one of those times she sneaked away from the mundane tending of her own family so that she could interfere deftly in ours. 'They have always been examples of perfect parenting…'

'I cannot find my socks!' Amar yelled from his room and whistled for the dog who did not respond and curled tightly on the foot-rug.

'It is still drying on the line,' Ma raised her voice too. ' Stop disturbing the dog when you want to talk to me.'

All this while I was rocking in a chair by the window, trying to match the sky's desolation with my own vacant look. Ma glanced in my direction but continued her discussion with Maasi, 'Almost perfect Meeta…you just heard the one who wants a dog to be his maid. He calls himself a social worker but cannot seem to help himself to his own socks which have been washed and dried by someone else.'

'It is a noble thing to do. Amar always thought of others before his own needs,' our aunt bravely tried on our behalf to brush away the doubts.

'Well, he has a job if nothing else. The other stays forever in the library. I think he has inherited his father's curse of trying all his life to do some monumental academic…' she broke off as if remembering something about that son, 'Arun!' she shouted again and turned to the dog out of habit. 'He is late for whatever he did not want to be late for – didn't the clock just strike eleven?' And then looking at me reproachingly, 'Somebody should have reminded him. I am now too old to take care of four adults.'

'He owns a watch with a functional alarm,' I said to the foot-rug and began chewing on the nail of my thumb.

Arun, for all his forgetfulness, always took cues better than the rest of us. He hobbled into the room – hobbled, because one shoe was still in the process of being slipped on – and smiled, but only at his mother. He dropped down on the floor to tug at the shoelaces. The dog quickly rolled on his back and stuck his legs up in the air for a tummy rub.

'I will be late tonight and won't be home for dinner,' Arun mumbled.

'Talk to me,' Ma said sternly, trying to catch his eye.

'I am,' he replied, still looking at the canine who had to now settle for a small pat on the side. Ma sighed.

'Don't wait up for me. I will use the key,' he said and stood up. The little physical attention motivated the dog to see him off till the door. They both ran into Anand who was just coming back from his computer classes.

'Hey mister! Care for a walk?' we heard him ask the dog.

'It is best to avoid the walk,' Arun offered his opinion. 'The weather report warned of sudden showers. Make do with the garden today.'

'Anand, drive your sister to the market. There's so much to do!' Ma shouted from her bed, 'The grocery list is stuck to the fridge…'

'He can do the shopping by himself,' I said.

'She can drive herself,' we heard Anand say.

'Perfect! How foolish of us to suppose that this was possible!' Ma fretted.

Maasi was making soothing noises, 'Go back to sleep. I will make sure they do whatever it is they have to do.' She tucked Ma into her blanket after helping her take medicines which we all knew had only one benefit – grogginess.

My eyes shut as if I were a clockwork doll that had been timed to fall asleep with Ma. Through closed eyelids, I could sense Maasi looking at me with exasperation before walking out to talk to Anand. From the way she tottered noisily in the hall I knew he had fled to the basement, probably locking the door with its big 'Get Out' sign. Soon a door shut softly and I knew the dog had taken her to the market.

And there I stood again in that same porch. The dog was a forgiving young sort when Ma was around but had no trouble turning into the pessimistic philosopher in his old age. All the talking must have taken its toll. He ignored me and sighed heavily. The room reeked of the night; the scents from the garden and its damp mud crammed the nostrils to subdue all other sensations.

'Don't you sleep anymore?' the voice startled me. Arun did not bother to look at me. It was a random sentence spoken to someone in a dream but I knew I was being addressed. There being no logic to sneaking on toe-tips anymore, I noisily dragged a heavily cushioned cane chair towards him and folded my feet as I sat down. I had a great dislike for sitting in chairs with dangling limbs where everything feels unhinged and ready to fall off. I hugged my knees tight with both hands.

'Or have you gone back to sleep walking?' he muttered.

If I did not reply to the first question, it was because the sarcasm forbade any. This one was tougher to ignore. I went back to chewing on the familiar nail of the thumb. The dog snored away gently. I had been found sleepwalking at regular intervals in my childhood, the most discussed event in the family was when one of the brothers found me standing on the balcony watching stars. He had pushed me back into my room but instead of going to bed I had taken the dog for a walk. It was almost two in the morning and whoever heard the gate creak had rushed out to rescue the drowsy animal.

'It is too warm. I cannot sleep,' I told him.

'Go to the basement. Anand has fixed a new air-conditioner for his equipment and usually works all night. You can use his bed.'

'What does he do there all the time?' I wondered aloud.

'What do any of us do?'

That ended the conversation. The dog's snore grew louder, willing us back to silence. I continued to sit out of sheer reluctance to pull myself away from that comfortable pose and looked out at the shadows of the thorny bushes beside the compound wall, the streetlight that only remained a pole since the bulb had fused a year ago, the tangled telephone wires, the roof of the house across the street and a tree that grew directly in the direction of our house like a pointed finger. Was the tree always there? How long does it take for a tree to take roots and spread on the shadowy landscape like that? I would have asked Arun but he was most likely to pretend to be asleep.

I got up to waddle back into the darkness of the house. My short crop of hair crinkled with a little static as I walked past the curtains and I put both my hands up to toss it back into its natural state of chaos. I would have perhaps walked back to my room but for the hopping voltage which noisily drew my attention to the fridge. A swig of cold water became tempting.

As usual, the fridge was mostly empty and so were the water bottles. I pulled open the freezer hoping for ice. Inside was a tall plastic glass of sundae with a slip of yellow post-it on the front. I pulled it out and held it against the bulb of the fridge – 'Dinner for 20th April. Anand'. The fierce scrawl implied 'nobody dare eat it but me' but of course no such thing needed to be said in a household where three grown up men lived together but rarely collided, a lot of which came from the disciplining the parents had agreed, disagreed and fought over. However, being the mutant, my rights and good behaviour were nobody's business but my own.

I pulled the little fold-up calendar over the fridge and held that too in the same light. Today was the twentieth but perhaps not yet the anointed dinner time. I put the calendar in the freezer out of a compulsion to replace what I had taken out, closing the fridge door softly. The sundae was frozen but had begun to sweat little beads of water in my palm. I pulled a spoon free from the sideboard and dug into it. Black currant and vanilla with plenty of unidentifiable nuts studded in – exotic and ordinary at the same time. Delightful! I headed back to my bed meaning to enjoy the ice cream as long as the heat would allow. It was an hour seething with unusual warmth, rising instead of cooling down as it progressed.

A shaft of light fell on me. The door of the basement was open and the figure at the door snorted in displeasure, 'It had to be you!' and then disappeared, unnerving me with the sudden exposure to an odious yellow light.

I always thought Anand more humane of the peas in the pod. Maybe it was because he kept secrets more effortlessly than the elder boys, both of whom had been coached to do nothing out of the regular and when they dared the slightest deviation, to come home and faithfully spill out the details. The compliance factor in the genes must have started to erode when Anand came around and totally disappeared when it was my turn.

It was destined to be a sleepless night and I was not averse to a little trip to the netherworld for that is what the basement was – a different orb, identified and claimed by Anand years ago. In the beginning, we all knew of his little missions, the little fixtures and alterations that came and went, but nobody could be bothered to keep tabs. He spent all his time under the floor, making little noises like a trapped rodent which Ma said was a comforting sign that he was not yet dead. So long as she was around and in bed, Anand made frequent appearances or tucked a note in the dog's collar for her to read. Very few of these notes were actually recovered and in various states of being chewed up. Ma put an end to that when, after much deliberation, she got an intercom installed and buzzed the domain below as she fancied. Her great fear was of being in some distorted state of dying and not finding any of us around to fetch the doctor. It was equally plausible to her mind, that Anand might be electrocuted by some of his outlandish gadgets and we would never know of it. A day after Ma died, I found the intercom dumped in the garbage can.

'Don't you sleep anymore?' Anand growled as I continued to spoon off the ice cream without remorse. I should have never troubled with that speech on differences between the brothers. Why do they have to ask even the same questions?

'Have you been looting an electronics shop?' I mumbled through a loaded mouth. The whole room was an intricate web of wires, gangly equipment that blinked coloured lights, bulky books sitting one atop another and then some more wires. Anand had his fits and bouts. I remember a time when the whole room looked like a sports centre with its ping pong table, the dart board on the wall, basketball, cricket and tennis gear all over the floor. A few months later it had all been cleared to make way for walls crammed with graffiti, books, newspaper clippings and large half-painted posters lying all around. The most interesting was the Zen phase when the basement turned empty but for a mat on the floor. Ma often sneaked over to see if the boy was doing drugs or coming down with some dreadful brain fever and once caught him sitting on the mat staring at a blank wall. She would go down every hour after that. He neither moved nor noticed her. Ma is known to have commented to her sister how Anand made even laziness look fashionable. That renunciation phase ended one day when the dog trotted into Ma's room with notice of a party in the basement for thirty boys. There was enough trash and beer bottles in the house the next morning to drown a Buddhist monastery.

'So, did you?' I persisted, still thinking of the possibility of theft. How long had it been since I had been down here? It certainly had been long enough for everything to look unrecognisable.

'No, I did not need to. I can afford it now,' he quietly bragged.

I wanted to sit down but the only chair in the room was occupied by clothes. I held out the half eaten dinner which Anand grabbed and continued the task I had so admirably begun. I swept the clothes to the top of a cardboard box and sat down to face a dark sinister computer on an overloaded table. It stared back, a small version of the larger tangle, little machines crisscrossed up like many kites hugging each other, all looking frightfully confusing to me.

'You have dug out all the black currant parts…' he complained.

'And you say all this pays you?' I was buying time until I could remember exactly what career path had been earmarked for him, 'What was it that you promised Ma you would study to be?'

'Yes, it pays. A lawyer'

'And this is all the work you do?' I insisted on knowing. Ma would have wanted me to, although I have not exactly been living up to her expectations myself. Did she know that this boy would straighten up after all and with a vengeance, making money and pursuing a career, lawyer or not, that he was not going to be counted as one of her failures?

Anand having braved past the melting vanilla, now settled back on his unkempt bed to enjoy the rest. 'I'm a software consultant,' he informed me.

'And who consults you?' I fidgeted in the chair. There was no space to pull up my feet and I realised how very cold the floor was. My cotton pyjamas gave up the fight as little goose bumps lined up on the skin. Perhaps it was his air-conditioner working unseen somewhere – the thought skimmed my mind. It suddenly felt very eerie, sitting there in the basement. A rat in a freezing sewer, with his wide rimmed glasses that did not catch any of the dim light from the lone bulb, Anand looked very dead. I stood up to go.

'...sometimes companies...sometimes individuals who don't want to pay corporate fees...sometimes friends...raising funds...building websites...gathering information...' he was speaking or so I was vaguely aware. I tripped over a fold of my pyjamas hurrying towards the soft warmth of the roof that my pulse quickened for now.

'Iti,' he called out softly when most of me had already made it above ground level. The brothers had a tendency to abbreviate my name – diti-iti-ti-ee – and how short it got always was a good indicator of how they felt, brevity suggesting affection.

'Hmmm?' I hummed cautiously.

'You are letting yourself go and that is not like you at all...' he said and I knew it was a killing effort. Anand had always been much less vocal with the advising as compared to the other two but the truth was that there was no Pa or Ma now; I was two years short of thirty, eating ice cream in my pyjamas and living with three unmarried older brothers who are rather odd themselves; I hadn't the foggiest idea what I was going to do the next day, leave alone the rest of my life.

'What would I have to do to be *like me*?' I asked and regretted the words coming out more earnestly than I meant them to. He was not ready to plunge in those torrential waters and stood silently at the door with a sad face.

'Well, sorry about your dinner…' I finally said and walked to the room by the stairs to visit my eldest brother. I had met two of them that night and decided to brave a third as well.

The door was shut and did not show any light through the slits. I knocked hard. It was a funny little room, built under the sweep of the stairs as if from the architect's guilt of not using every odd space of the building. Under that sloppy uneven roof Amar had made his burrow, refusing to take our quiet suggestions that he move into Ma's large spacious room when she died. He was the tallest, and in certain corners of the odd room, he had to slouch while standing up, but every nook which he refused to either abandon or alter had long been part of his own steady nature.

I knocked with my feet the second time and heard scampering on the other side. He opened the door and even in the dark knew it to be me. 'Have you started to debate on the need to sleep now?' he growled and turned on a little light by the door.

I sat down on the bed. Amar resignedly started to look for his glasses. One rarely saw him without them. During days when Maria was still in charge of bathing us, he would fight like a man to keep his glasses knowing the futility of the whole effort and the inevitable separation. It was perhaps the only time Maria would thump him on the back, not hard enough to invite Ma's censure – she liked to thrash her kids herself – but not soft enough to keep him from feeling belittled. It was the only individualistic deed of his childhood: starting a campaign to be considered responsible enough for his own wash. I had hardly made it to school then, and Maria being a gentle ally, the whole controversy was just plain amusement that did not directly affect my routine. I do remember the spectacle of Amar standing bravely in a bath towel explaining his rights to our mother. Surprisingly he got permission to bathe himself but I never heard him argue with Ma again as far as my recollection goes.

Amar had always kept his room incredibly spic and sorted, almost frugal. Three large wall posters dominated the space – one of a baby tiger crouching behind big font that begged he be saved, the other two were of very poor children who must have very little to grin about as they did in the pictures. Amar had clicked each of those, copies of which, probably thousands, had made it to distant walls. The cub was born in a zoo and the children had just been treated to free ice cream, much like me that night.

I leaned a little towards a pillow and again felt the static crawl across my head. Amar flattened my hair this time and because I had not said a word, I looked at him with surprise. His hands awkwardly came down on his knees in response.

'You look just like Pa,' I thought aloud.

Amar must have heard it a thousand times before. He was all Pa – just bigger, hairier and wearing thicker glasses, but he still raised an eyebrow in surprise and went about earnestly putting his own tousled hair in order. Looking at him, that flitting instant, I missed the parent who did everything possible to avoid any initiative towards small talk. Ma juggled all the words while Pa chased the greatness that was sure to elude him.

'Pa would have wanted you to be more responsible with your life,' he was getting straight to business.

'And what would that be?' I snapped, tired of being patronised by all three of them that night.

He did not expect my sharp retort and groped for the right words, 'Be responsible...plan your life...build a career ...'

'Hah!' I scoffed and got up to go, 'and is doing charity profitable?' I thought I was justified in asking. He was the one who started the attack on personal choices.

'Almost...' he said, now soft and engrossed, just like Pa would when he wanted us to disappear from his sight, 'You would be surprised but doing good for people pays a little...'

The dog gave out a few sharp barks and it echoed in the empty house. I jumped. Amar pushed me gently outside the door and I rolled obligingly like a kitten. 'Don't worry. He has a fixation on the cat next door. She knows he is locked up at night and sits on the compound wall just to spite him,' he explained and before any more could be said, shut the door on my face. I was left with no option but to return to my own bed.

21

I HAD SOMEHOW FAILED TO UNDERSTAND THE SECRET formula the brothers had hit upon for a peaceful co-existence. Even the dog had managed to fit in despite having to endure conversations he never began. Not too long before the eventful night just remembered, I woke up to find myself an obstruction in their lives, saying all the wrong things, trampling upon schedules with little deference for privacy. I sat down on the front steps to gaze at the sky in perfect peace; that day, I decided not to go to work or do my share of chores in the house; a few weeks later, I stopped having my bath or looking into a mirror, till the untidiness could not be explained as eccentricity anymore. Nothing seemed so essential anymore. I ate when the hunger got unbearable but more from necessity than anything else. Often I stayed in bed, doing what I liked best – nothing. And I was happy. If only the rest of the world knew how easy it was to stop doing everything that compels us. It was liberating with absolutely no way of explaining how immensely so! In the beginning I was habituated to some thinking but soon that seemed such an encumbrance. So I sat and purged my life, of all the routine activities, of thoughts, of feelings, of aspirations and above all, that greatest shackle of them all – faith, unless believing in nothing can qualify to be one.

Two weeks of this blissful existence was too much for my brothers to endure. They began to cart me to the doctors, a bevy of them. I rolled my feet up and refused to co-operate. It was an important time for me and something was surely being born out of that hollow. An identity. A desire. What am I? – came the words from the abyss within. An artist – was the answer. I smiled and my brothers whined collectively at my misfortune.

The Big House, they explained, was like a holiday home – expensive (but who cares when one's only sister is losing her mind?) and comfortable. I could rest plenty while good people kept an eye on me all the time. That also meant they could return to their routines in peace. It was interesting how they called it 'the place', 'the house', even 'the boarding' – anything but what the presence of so many white uniforms would have merited it to be.

If on any regular sunny day, you are to trudge the eleven kilometres from the nearest town to here, not for lack of a road but infrequent public transport, you would be greeted with blank or blinking eyes when asked for the 'sanatorium'. Try saying 'the big house' and fingers will rise immediately to poke an imaginary point in the green hills. Even more interesting is how the same ignorance is encouraged within the house, everyone pretending that they are here to toast a drink to the fresh breeze and have a frolicking vacation before tumbling back to the plains. Well, illusions are fine by me, sometimes even mandatory. If asked, I say that I am as comfortable as any person in a doctor's waiting room, heavy with an undiagnosed ailment but joyous to be on the verge of finding out what it can possibly be.

22

MA WAS A 'DO-ER' AND THE BOYS HAVE LEARNT THAT FROM her. It was better – she insisted – to keep working even if it is very little, as long as it gave the pretence of much. To stay still for even a moment was a risk of being considered extinct. She was just as prompt to use the cane on us as the dreaded chalk missiles on her students when they paid little attention. The chemistry lab assistant in her department once confided to me, when I had strayed over on some errand, that even the beakers seemed to quake as she peered at the concoctions presented to her. O yes, Ma was an action figure of considerable esteem.

Pa said – think, and keep thinking, and that is the only way you will get any respect at all. It was yet unknown to him that the tag of an intelligent man would drag him to ultimate despair and obscurity. As the years passed, he became one with the dusty maps and files in the history department and students had to frequently endure his pausing in the middle of lectures to stare at the ceiling as if the most innovative of ideas were sitting there saluting him. Pa never realised when he gave up on the thinking. But Ma always stayed a do-er.

I had decided early to ignore both their convictions with equanimity. It marked me out for constant scrutiny and monitoring.

'The girl is entirely rustic. I am never even sure that she is mine. We should have stopped at three children,' Ma said as often as it was possible to do so without blunting the sting. She had an audience that day in our Maasi and her husband.

'She is restless and eager to learn,' explained our father peering at the four of us over his glasses. When I did not think of him as 'Pa', I saw in him the faces of all the history teachers I had known, weighed under a legacy of boredom – learn all the dates that had ever erred into allowing something of consequence to take place, remember the good kings who built ugly buildings or got trees planted on both sides of the road and the bad ones who drank themselves silly or chopped heads for sport with a rounded reference to how demanding or distinct the political weather of those times had been. Something of all that had hastened the process of Pa turning into a sceptic, though he explained often that I ought not to put him in the same league as my moronic teachers with elementary degrees, for he was an academician, a scholar. To me, young as I was, and perhaps even now, it was all the same.

'She reminds me so much of you,' Maasi said kindly.

Ma choked on her toast. 'Maria! Maria!' she shouted. 'Have you emptied the gutter beside our road?'

Maria blinked. She was a good person, a simpleton really, and an unlikely candidate for sarcasm. 'Gutter?' she invariably waited for further instructions.

'No, don't bother. I see you have already poured it to us as coffee,' Ma muttered as her blue pen struck around another boring but incisive analysis in the day's newspaper. Maria wrung her hands nervously before picking up four schoolbags. She would have opted for a leather flogging to Ma's dense taunts, but luckily it was time for us to go out and be rescued by the school bus.

'They should carry their own schoolbags, Maria. You know that,' Pa was surprisingly quick to notice, and the bulging sacks were promptly hoisted on us.

'It is Janmashtami today. Hasn't your school declared a holiday?' said the aunt's husband. I wished he had said that an hour ago when Maria had dragged me out of bed holding my toes. She knew some exquisite torture methods which worked when her gentle squeaky voice failed. I almost dashed back to bed at the suggestion of a holiday while the brothers, despite the full-time occupation of being model children, acted human for a change. They quickly slid their bags onto the floor where mine had already sprawled out to relax.

'The trouble with this country is too many holidays. How does it matter if it were Independence Day or some vague ritual of some vaguer tribe? We only use it to amuse ourselves and waste another perfectly good working day,' Pa grumbled.

'Pick up your bags and go to the bus stop. If the bus does not turn up, then come home,' said Ma surveying her troops.

'...then come home and I will take you to school in a cab,' added Pa. He could not accept a holiday for some festival we had no intention of celebrating. I think if he took us to school and found the place padlocked, he would leave us behind to guard and polish the iron gates.

Ma picked another toast and scraped it hard with the butter knife. She liked her bread toasted to a particular crustiness that the toaster never managed to please her with. Maria had instructions to nearly burn the bread so that Ma could scrape the dark portions with great diligence until it was an even corroded brown. One thing I have in common with the brothers, perhaps the only thing now, is our loathing of bread in any form, especially toasted. They see it as an evil epitome of everything imperfect in this world. I see it as inedible and only fit for scrapping.

'Let them stay at home,' our good hearted aunt pleaded, 'I see so little of them and anyway we are leaving tomorrow.'

Ma, who had grown up bullying her sister, did not intend to change her ways. She put her toast down, 'If they were yours, mark my words, they would be auctioning you off right this moment at some village fair. There is such a thing as "too good" my dear. Ratan is right – all they do is go to school and what is the point if they can't do that right? Did the teachers say anything about a holiday?' she directed the last question at the brothers, ignoring me who was as certain to lie as her little men would swear by the truth.

'Yes,' whispered I, hoping to inspire the boys.

'No,' volunteered Amar for the rest of us. We had a poor spokesman and the bags had to be hitched again. I found their compliance sickening and slowly slid my feet out of my shoes. The vile things were biting my flesh through the socks. But why blame the shoes? The brutes who ran my school had neither sense of fashion nor comfort. I ran a count on my fingers and nothing much had changed since the last calculations – there were another eight years of school to endure. The thought made me mad but I fought the temptation to jump at Amar. My parents, who expected impeccable manners from us even while we played games, were even more particular about our manners in company. They had many theories on upbringing and parenting, most of which any child in her right mind would boycott. Sadly, I had the misfortune of being at the heels of three who bent to every word. Maria was already hustling us out like we were chicken let loose in her courtyard.

'We could all go to Appu Ghar and have a day of fun!' said Maasi who, I am sure can be gleaned by now, had no children of her own. The amusement park came to mind – the colourful giant wheels, giddy rides with whimsical names and a huge swinging ship – it was a pilgrimage for the young. I came close to speaking out in favour of a swap of mothers. My aunt would know what to do with a girl. At that very moment, however, she was being intimidated by icy silence from both my parents who would not condescend to respond to such barbaric suggestions.

'Go, go, go,' Pa muttered and bent his head. He looked very tired and defeated suddenly. His fingers dropped lifeless on the table, lying like they had been severed, before moving again to unsteadily hook the handle of a cup. Alarmed, we began to scurry on.

'The boys are a lot like you,' the uncle placated my mother. The owner of a very successful hardware business, he was also in charge of making repairs whenever his wife spoke her mind and that was certainly the right thing to say.

Ma beamed at him, 'Well, that they are...'

'I just remembered...you were so sure that Aditi would be a boy too!' the aunt was bouncing back in action.

Ma's face darkened again. She hated surprises and I had been just that.

Ma thought of her life as a finished picture on the wall, all the details already there if anyone would care to see – there was her, and there was Ratan shining radiant as a true original thinker the world had declared itself useless without, and standing around them were four smart promising boys. No, not three boys and one girl. She was sure there would be four of the same gender. That my father also never quite turned out as he was in the picture is another matter to be examined later.

Pa smiled, 'You remember well Meeta! She had said – what will I do with a girl?' and then wilted under Ma's glare. His nose, however, continued to quiver as it did when he perceived anything with great merriment.

This was all hitherto unknown information to me. My brothers were already on their way out but I lingered. Ma watched me from the corner of her eyes. I knew she was registering that I had dissent in my blood. I had chosen to be a girl. I could almost sense the cane behind the door listening just as keenly.

'But I am sure you are glad now. She is adorable! Girls are so much more gentle and attached to their parents,' Maasi beamed. She was wrong about me but I would have kissed her hand in quiet gratitude if Maria had not grabbed the collar of my shirt just as the bus turned around the bend of our road.

'What children really need is to spend their childhood in a good strict hostel. You learn to get no special privileges and to do without emotional crutches. I remember when I was in hostel...' the uncle began.

'Meeta! You are lucky to be married to such a sensible man. I completely agree. Success in later life can always be traced to childhood training…' Ma had found the voice of her soul in another throat.

'Oh yes! He is such an achiever! He plans to expand the family business, specialise in toilet stuff,' Maasi felt obliged to add an appreciation she did not feel – I can always tell.

'Designer sanitary ware,' the man firmly corrected her and turned to Ma, 'although I am sure a hostel can never take the place of a mother's impressive personality.'

'Taps is the business to be in,' insisted our father, 'the good taps are always ugly and the pretty ones are so inconvenient and unaffordable for regular folk like us.'

'For the children, Ratan, hostel would be a good experience,' Ma affirmed.

'The children….' Pa mused for while and then remembering us, 'they will be fine here. Better the fear of parents than a thrashing from some frustrated stranger.'

'Words of wisdom!' Maasi nodded her appreciation. She thought highly of her sister's husband, perhaps even wished she had married someone like him.

The bus honked loudly at the gate. The only other thing I remember of that morning is Maria's lips close to my ears while I clambered into the bus. She said, 'None of that matters now. Forget it.'

23

ONE MOMENT, STRAPPED TO OUR BACKS – PROBABLY THE only one deserving of being a memory but kept from us – is that of our birth. An intense emergence, uncurling from a curved squishy foetus into a child with flaying limbs. What had it felt like? What was that comforting darkness that one had to be exiled from? What was the sensation of the new light like? If I could choose anything to revisit from the past, I would have wanted it to be the day I was born, the very instant even.

Pa must have said – How bad can a daughter be?

Ma must have snapped – I wanted another boy.

We have three – Pa no doubt would have tried to reason.

Ma would have mentally scanned the finished picture on the wall of her mind – no, no girl. She had nothing against babies born as girls, and certainly none of the conventional objections that ran as rapids in the vast waters of her society. It was nothing more than a simple but vital discrepancy in the picture she had hung up in her mind. There was no girl in it but I had turned up nonetheless, somehow giving her the surprise she did not care to have.

24

YEARS LATER, AFTER PA DIED WHILE WATCHING A BOISTEROUS television show, I was chosen to sort out his drawer in the study. I found among many things – scores of files with elaborate labels on their faces but empty within, an apple bitten into before being forgotten, a box of biscuits that had been converted into a colony of ants, little books of verse hidden under many layers of paper for being the shameful indulgence it was considered and pens that did not write – a faded colourless photograph of a young woman printed in a newspaper.

I kept the clipping in my jacket instead of dumping it into the big box that held the rest of the clutter and looked at it again later as I was peeling my clothes off in the bath. The young woman in the picture was carrying a grimy little girl in the middle of a rain-washed slum, the pleats of her sari hitched high in the other hand and making her way through a puddle. She was watched by many admiring people, all as untidy as their dismal houses. In the background were faint outlines of other women, all dressed in dark sarees and short-sleeved light blouses. The young woman held the child as if it was a precious thing dropped from heaven she had simply happened to catch. There was a rare serenity in her eyes. I looked for a date on the little newspaper scrap but found none. The caption mentioned the name of a women's organisation. It seemed familiar but that might also be attributable to all the socialistic speeches the campus kept echoing with or the many fiercely articulate friends that Ma invited for dinner, the ones we were not allowed to listen to.

Is this all there is? – I think that is what Ma said when I dragged the cardboard box from Pa's room to the porch for the street-sweeper to take with him. What did she expect? Pa had started to shred papers since months, sometimes even clothes; anything he thought was disposable, which for the most part implied everything. He would sit down to write and read and work every morning, the door of the study tightly shut to all of us. By noon, someone would knock and enter with his lunch to find him intent at the task of destruction. An involved zealous look is all he spared to·wave the tray towards a untidy table, as we stood stunned by the sight of him busily tearing sheaves of paper, till told to go away and not break his concentration at work.

And then Ma still finds it in her to say — Are you sure you have cleared all his stuff out? Is this all there is?

I suppose I could have told her about the clipping but it did not seem like the kind of thing that would matter to her. Or if it did, why did she not directly ask me if I had seen some faded woman on some faded piece of paper walking through a puddle in a slum? Was that what she really wanted to find out?

A few days later when I wore the same jacket and slipped my hand into the pocket, the paper was gone. I never gave it another thought.

Again, when Ma died, the dreary task of clearing her papers was imposed on me, which goes to show that the passing of the years leave some things unchanged. I found that same newspaper clipping in her drawer — not under old forgotten papers but in the sandal-fragrant nook of her dresser where she kept empty bottles of perfumes. It was only then I recognised the woman in the picture. She was my mother.

It was a great discovery, the only one I had made so far worth sharing with others. I marched into the study where Amar and Arun sat over Pa's now empty table and played chess. Anand was sitting by the window puffing at a cigarette greedily — his first within the house. I explained about the tattered clipping that kept turning up in the drawers of dead parents. They nodded at me politely.

'Pa fell in love with her when he saw the picture. You know how idealistic he was…or maybe you don't remember…you were so little then. He used to say there is so much goodness in the world. ' Anand coughed and spoke between cigarette puffs.

I was aghast and said, 'He told me to trust nobody and that no favour came without an expectation attached to it.'

'I told you this was long ago, around the time Pa had joined his department. Ma was quite revolutionary those days. She was full of radical ideals and very involved in social work. They had never met even though she was teaching in the same campus.'

'Really?' I wondered. What had been a remarkable discovery was apparently family-lore minus my knowledge.

'Of course! He got Sundar uncle to introduce them and they were married that very week. Pa said it was the only time the world had seemed to move faster than what books claimed. By the end of the year, he was already a father,' said Amar referring to his own birth.

'Ah!' I was a little confused about how they seemed to know the story so well while I was hearing it for the first time.

'There is a secret though,' said Anand lighting a fresh cigarette on the ends of the dying one. I was itching to risk a puff myself but did not want to divert from an interesting tale. 'The secret is that Ma for some reason never went back to volunteer for that organisation and Pa never told her that he had seen her picture in the newspaper.'

'And how do you know that?' Amar asked sharply. Arun arched his back away from the chess board. I finally had some company in ignorance.

He smiled. 'I was the one who found the clipping in Iti's jacket and took it to Ma. She told me a little of that brief love story and the rest I got from Sundar uncle.'

We were quiet. I suddenly felt insanely jealous of the frail dirt-streaked girl in the picture who was looking at Ma's face. I wished I was that girl.

'I guess it was his own childish indulgence. Most couples have secret fantasies – this was his. I think he didn't like the idea that the woman he married was the one he had fallen in love with. Or maybe Ma was not in reality what this picture had led him to believe. Who knows? It made Ma happy though, to know he had kept the picture.'

'Maybe it is because he loved her,' I said feebly. They all looked at me surprised. I was not one to talk of such unfounded sentiments. 'A wild guess,' I mumbled to cover my embarrassment.

Anand flicked some ash onto the window grills and it stayed there undecided on which side of the window to fall as the wind blew. These little things irritate me and must be one of those quirks a mother bequeaths her daughter without either of them knowing it. I went over and blew on the ash. It drifted into the garden outside. My brothers were looking at me curiously. I always showed more passion for the inanimate than the living. They knew that. So, why stare?

'I will break your fingers one by one if you ever touch my jacket without my permission again,' I snarled at Anand.

Anand doused his cigarette again on the grill, leaving it there for dramatic effect and winked at me. Till that time, I never thought of the four of us as odd even though every single person who knew us said so. But seeing the three of them (while they watched me), and holding an old piece of newspaper in my hands, I knew there had to be something different about all of us.

The other two had already started a fresh game. The pawns scrambled around for their rightful place. A rook, unable to bear the commotion, surreptitiously rolled off the table.

'There is nothing much to clear out of Ma's belongings. She had sorted and labelled them herself. There is a pile which does say "burn". So we can have a bonfire in the garden tonight,' I announced.

'Thank you my dear. I shall bring the wine,' Amar said with mock-gallantry.

I handed him the newspaper article. 'For extra fuel…' I said and stomped out. I never asked him about it again.

Chinese food had been ordered and delivered home by a Nepali boy whose uncle had been cooking inside 'The Golden Dragon' for as long as we could remember. We ate sitting around the embers when someone had the bright idea of throwing pieces of wood lying in the garage. The fire glowed long after all the paper became smoke. The noodles were cold worms and the chillies in the chicken were ferocious but we felt liberated. There was not a soul left to tell us what to do or what not to.

After a while, someone began to push the paper boxes which the food had come in towards the fire. We added the leftovers from our plates over that, solemnly, as if witch doctors at a special brewing.

Almost at midnight, when everything burning had charred itself out and the stars watched us coldly, I thought I saw tears running down the faces of my brothers. Instinct made me touch my own face. It was a little wet. A flash of lightning lit up the sky behind the dark buildings and I stood up to announce the drizzle. We went inside, very quietly, looking for our beds.

25

The Lord made everything for a purpose,
Even the wicked for an evil day.
— THE HOLY BIBLE (Prov. 16:1-4)

THE EVENTS AND TRIBULATIONS AT THE RED-BRICK SCHOOL might have implied that I escaped education, but it had only been a charming prelude to the real nightmare that followed. Not sure if I had been kicked out of school or if I had willingly renounced it, I was nonetheless at the mercy of Ma's whims. She brushed aside any apprehensions Pa voiced about sacrificing children to an alien culture and marched me off to the nearest missionary school, from where some of her friends swore their children had emerged with unmistakable polish. I learnt it was an all-girls institution and that in itself was a punishment. I had a certain fondness for boorish boys and revelled in their company after all the time I had to spend with my docile and inspid brothers. To take ribbons, ironed pleated-skirts, giggles, ankle-socks and ridiculous film star crushes for the rest of my schooling was like a life sentence that would never end. There is just as much to say about the nuns rustling around in stiff starched habits and unmasked disapproval in their eyes. Well, maybe it is too harsh to brand the whole sisterly lot thus. I am going to save myself that trouble and go straight to the more hardened ones or rather the one ordeal that awaited me in the new school.

Sister Judith was so tough that even Ma shrank in stature from the encounter. I joined the new school in the middle of a semester due to the unavoidable circumstances already mentioned, and on account of my troublesome past was handed over to Sister Judith.

'She has a mind of her own,' Ma said gently. I admit to having been taken aback at not hearing the usual details of my many misdemeanours. 'I am sure you will guide her...' That would be the closest Ma ever came to portraying me as an angel.

Sister Judith did not wait to hear the rest. She tucked both hands under the front flap of her habit, a sorcerer in a freshly starched cape on the verge of an earth shaking spell. 'Come here, child,' she said to me in a raspy voice, ignoring Ma altogether which is no mean achievement. I walked over with great veneration: nobody else I knew had ever managed to step over that formidable mother of mine.

'Yes ma'am,' I muttered.

'I am Sister Judith,' she corrected me, the ignoramus from the government school who had evidently not encountered a woman in habit ever before. I blushed. 'The last room down this corridor is your classroom. Take a seat in the first row and write an essay on why you are changing your school mid-term. In two pages. No fat sprawling letters and no scattering the words to fill up the ruled lines. You will soon learn that I know all the tricks of the trade. Write me an honest essay and let me see how much English you know.'

I tried to look at her shoes. Pa would have insisted. He said a person with tight shoes was always ruthless. I only saw the straight edge of her habit but was sure that her toes were cramped into pulpy disarray. Ma was nudging me in the direction of the classroom. I obliged. Behind me, I could hear my new teacher extolling how all children needed to know that they would never achieve anything in life if they did not work hard when young. Ma weakly continued on what a good kid I was at heart, something that a little flogging would easily reveal. I had tears in my eyes from hearing her say something good about me and hesitated outside the dreaded classroom.

'I believe that children can be disciplined in ways other than a physical punishment,' I heard the Sister say and the heart sank. She was no doubt more lethal than all the other disciplinarians I had encountered before, using a cane that I could neither see nor anticipate. That first day in her class froze my spirits for the rest of time spent in the school. It would never matter again whether I studied with thousands of girls or mutilated lab monkeys. Survival preceded all. When I sat down as directed, I found everyone busily and nervously scribbling into their books. It was a moment of insight into a topsy-turvy world. I had never before seen a room filled with children sitting in perfect decorum when no authority was looming large. Not so long ago, I had had the pleasure of being in the company of those who hooted and pranced even in the presence of the teacher, despite the dire risk of ending up on the bench with a peon who looked capable of hunting them down and killing them.

I did not write any essay. It was harrowing to sit at the front of the class, a position I have held before with equal distaste. Luckily for me, the Sister walked into the room and noticed one of the girls who had dared turn up with a slight suggestion of make-up on her face.

'Mala! Come here child!' The veins at her temples were beginning to stand out and her voice shook with anger, 'Are you a butterfly child?' Incidentally, Sister Judith knew the art of saying 'child' like she meant 'psychotic serial-killer'. The girl summoned thus looked willing to lop her head off and fling it from the window if it would have helped escaping that moment, but she only trembled and clutched her desk tight.

A million afternoons later, out shopping for socks, I ran into this same Mala at the corner of a nameless street holding a harried little boy by his hair. As she subdued her son's hysterical cries, she waved enthusiastically at me. Mala remembered my first day in Sister Judith's class for it had also been her birthday. Her mother, guilty of spending whole days in beauty parlours – not getting pampered but earning a livelihood from waxing legs – had gifted her a little cosmetic kit, which explained Sister Judith's discovery. Mala told me she had not touched any colour to her face since then, so traumatised had she been by the experience. We both saw the scene re-enacted in each other's eyes, said quick goodbyes, and walked in opposite directions never to meet again.

Sister Judith calmly asked the beet-red girl who had dared paint her birthday face, 'Which writer did you write your essay on?'

'Charles Dickens,' the girl could barely speak.

'Speak up child! Chickens?!'

'De...Dickens...'

'Read it out aloud to the class. And please stand here beside me. Let everyone have a good look at your bu-tt-er-fly face.'

The girl coughed and spluttered through the pages that trembled in her hands. There was fearful silence in the room as Sister Judith continued to scrutinise the girl from head to toe. The essay was truly heading for trouble. That it had been neatly copied from the back notes of some text book was obvious even to me. Full of words and phrases the girl could barely pronounce, there were references to some works which even Dickens would forget having written. There was long silence when Mala stopped reading.

Sister Judith said in an even death knell, 'Don't you have a brain, child? Or did you leave it behind at home?'

The poor girl cringed in fear, the tears stinging her eyes.

'This here,' the Sister said, leaning forward to take the book from trembling hands 'is a masterpiece and rightfully a property of the school that tolerates the likes of you.' She slammed the notebook on the table. 'You sit down right now and write me another essay. Perhaps you would care to enlighten us on one character of your choice from any of Dickens's novels that you seem to have studied so extensively. I want the essay submitted before the end of this hour.'

I watched the girl's painted face flush into a bizarre shade of lavender. Sister Judith must have noticed too for she said, 'But first, you need to wash your face and if you again wish to be a rainbow, stay in the garden, don't come to my class.'

The girl fled but not before carefully shutting the door behind her. I was soon to learn that the Sister was particular that the door to her classroom remained closed. She probably took delight in the fact that there was no visible escape route. We were trapped in her head and in that room. It was a miserable claustrophobic feeling, one that quickly returns to my heart even as I remember it now. I had got an effective demonstration of the woman's idea of taming us to total submission. No physical violence: just an attitude – worse than the caning and ten times more frightful. Mala never returned from the bathroom during that hour and was not missed.

Sister Judith had an hour with us each day and for over a month she did not notice me apart from calling my name from her register to which I quickly said 'present' before she could look up for a face to match it with. The anonymity was a relief and gave me time to get used to the rest of the carnival. I was still jittery about being amidst so many girls in one place.

Schooling after that was not entirely the calamity I might have made it out to be. There were some good souls who slaved hard to make us think beyond our books or the blackboard, some who even managed to turn inscrutable formulae into something sensible. And though not all the teachers were nuns, they were all women except for the yoga teacher and he was far too intimidated by the others to stand out as a man.

Ma and Pa watched me in the evenings like hawks, for any sign of subdued acceptance if not rebellion. I stoutly refused to talk about school. They had made their choice and I would live it like it was my own. Soon they were content to simply monitor my journey through each exam. A whole world of peace lay between getting 34 or 36 marks on the report card. Except for one silly math test, I managed to stay with the redeeming 36 which would be written in green ink instead of the red 34 or the blue 35. Being colour blind could have been exceedingly liberating in those circumstances, but since that was not to be, Pa and Ma scrutinised every single mark on the brothers' cards while just running an eye over mine hoping it would be all green. Very quickly I learnt enough tricks to manage just that.

The brothers were pleased that the only disgrace of their spotless lives was gone from the red-brick school. With my exit, they were able to relish the praises over their many achievements without shame of having the rest of the school know they were related me.

I continued to strike my own discordant notes at home and encountered both the parental canes very often but never discussed school, not even when curiosity led the family to ask. At the few parent–teacher meetings, Ma went full of anticipation only to be ignored in favour of those girls who were sure to do mankind proud or those whose brains rejected education. I was neither.

'Mediocrity!' Pa finally announced at the dinner table one evening after one such long meeting when a teacher had struggled to remember my face despite their spelling out my name, 'that is what we had failed to comprehend. Our child is mediocre,' he sighed.

The brothers all turned to look at me. I chewed on a fish bone and felt cheerful. Their compulsion to give my innovative behaviour a name was understandable and pardonable. The important thing, it was clear to me, was that I had found a way to beat the system and not be castigated for it.

26

MARIA WAS THE ONLY ONE AT HOME WHO TRIED TO participate in my life behind those tall school walls that were spiked with broken glass. Meant to keep trespassers out, it also kept me in. The two stocky men at the gate were not convinced about looking the other way when an unhappy child strolled out to freedom. Maria knew one of the maids who worked in the convent attached to the school, a diminutive knob-kneed girl with a perpetual cold, called Nimmi. Having been brought there from a nearby village by very pious but poor parents, she stayed in the servant quarters and rarely ventured out.

Nimmi started her career in the convent kitchen cutting vegetables till one of the supervisors who had a great fear of germs caught her sneezing while dicing a potato. Nimmi was soon mopping floors. Someone then reported a missing pendant – a gold cross studded with diamonds, they kept repeating for years thereafter – so Nimmi was scuttled off to water and tend the vegetable patch where the assault of sun-rain-dust worsened her delicate constitution. Nimmi was left with no choice but to make herself useful in the school administrative office. She was put in charge of sorting the mail, moving files and stocking chalk in the classrooms but it was the special assignment of ringing the school-bell at the end of every hour that gave her a special glow. One of the teachers gifted an old wrist watch which she grew exceedingly attached to, looking at it ever so often. Nimmi wore her watch even in bed. Maria told me so.

Nimmi and Maria made unlikely friends. Maria needed to keep tabs on me. Nimmi wanted to know of life outside the convent where one could converse with young men without censure and go to the movies. Maria did not omit any details of her escapades and might have even added some from her own imagination. By the end of a year of friendship, Nimmi had eloped with the watchman on night duty at the convent. He was sixty-five-years old, limp in one leg and had three runny-nosed children from a first wife who had died under mysterious circumstances. The nuns were aghast but agreed to let them both continue with their jobs after copious tears had been shed by the newly-weds. Nimmi continued to move us from one hour to another, one subject to another, her bell shrill and rung with such precision that one could time not only when the bell started to ring but also when it fell silent – exactly eight seconds later.

Nimmi dwindled away after her boldest adventure, the one that had fetched an abusive old husband, but continued to ring the bell with a faded sort of pride. Maria soon began to avoid her.

During that year of their friendship, I stayed in school but had turned invisible. Maria knew I was attending all my classes. She also knew — Nimmi was a diligent reporter — that I was never caught or punished or made to wait on any bench outside any room. I was turning into a model child too like the boys, but on my own terms. Unknown to all, including Maria, a fine plan was being executed behind the whole facade. I sat through all my classes, wrote enough in the notebooks to spare me punishment or shame for not doing any studying but at the same time put such minimal effort that they merely got accepted as the efforts of a dunce. I attended all the sports trials and played so badly nobody wanted me on any team. I sat in the shade and laughed at the fools who sweated and competed and ended up getting pushed around the field by hefty seniors. I auditioned for all the cultural events too and the same floppy act bailed me out again. I ended up a spectator but a bad one because I did not like to clap. The rest of my school years sailed past. Mediocrity, I decided by then, suited me just fine.

Maria never said anything to me about her chats with Nimmi but she must have given a good account to my parents who agreed that I deserved more fresh air and relaxation. They suggested park outings. Instead Maria began to take me with her to the movies in the afternoons. Often we were joined by her young male friends. I was proving to be a serious movie-goer and a reliable collaborator, while she had new sensations under her clothes.

27

TELLING A STORY LIKE THIS DRAINS THE LIFE OUT OF ME, strands of thought constantly collapsing from the exertion of challenging a weak memory. To tell the events of one's own life when it has probably not even been half-lived, is probably pointless. But then, how am I to know where I stand in the story? At the half-way mark? Or just one step away from the end? If I am closer to the beginning, there is still hope that this might turn out to be something of consequence.

The best stories are set in times of strife, insisted Nandita; as with our freedom struggle, a nation's identity rising from the dust of the departing colonisers. Or it could be about days of nostalgia, when kings and warriors and breathtakingly beautiful princesses fell in love, battled for pride and died for immorality. Better still, those that feed entirely on fantasy, gods and demons and heavenly damsels in a world of mythical creatures, the powers of benevolence waging that enduring war against the powers of meanness. Those are the best stories, Nandita said.

What can a story with neither cause nor conviction possibly say? What mountains, on earth or in minds, can it possibly move? Why bother narrating that story?

The university campus being a stronghold of progressive thought and socialist passions might seem the sort of place to spin enough causes for one to feel strongly about. Indeed, I have been a witness to frequent demonstrations, all carried out with equal sincerity whether for the rights of nesting Ridley turtles or displaced Tibetans. As for the bad governance by the people picked from amongst us, everyone complained while equivocally conceding that a few decades of self-rule were not enough to bring back the golden ages. It was an ambivalent political atmosphere that had the peculiar effect of making one believe that this was all there was to life as a citizen – protest and then reconciliation.

We still had those wars and nuclear tests. We were still being mocked, molested and raped. We had the violence of the forgotten people who just wanted to be heard. We saw mayhem in consciences as the corrupt flourished. We felt shame in being simple and honest. We silently melted into a common indifference and fatalistic acceptance.

Pa never went to any meeting that had overtones of controversy. He was afraid it would put brakes on his research work which depended on everyone from the office typist to the bureaucrat in the ministry for survival. Ma had her own meetings but we never knew where they took place or with whom. All we knew was that she left with a smile and came back in pain.

There is no real story unless there is a real cause. All tales, like these, born in the times of cause-less-ness are like beating a drum with a ruptured face.

I am beating that drum. I am beating it as best as I can.

28

'SHE HAS NO HANDWRITING,' MRS JINDAL EXPLAINED patiently to Ma.

'What do you mean? She is literate, isn't she? She can read and she can write,' Ma bristled back.

Mrs Jindal, experienced and accustomed to dealing with parents in denial, merely pushed back her chair. She had taken over when Sister Judith had let us, the mentally battered bunch, haul ourselves onto the next grade and there were significant differences in their approach. While the unflagging nun was constantly on a crusade, Mrs Jindal's manner of teaching the English language was mostly leaving things to chance. She waded through the pages of the text at her own pace. A hippo with arthritis might have fared better, but considering that we had just slipped out of Sister Judith's clutches, it was not our lot to complain. Some of us, Mrs Jindal presumed, possibly learnt something that would be retained till the examination day and she was uncannily right about that. Not being pressurised into learning grammar and poetry was any day better than having it drilled through our skulls. We miraculously remembered all that was forgettable.

If Mrs Jindal cared strongly about anything, we never found out. She was amicable on her worst day and absentmindedly indulgent on her best. She rambled through the lessons and forgot all about us the instant Nimmi rang her sacrosanct bell. But for certain precedents laid down by Sister Judith herself, our matronly Mrs Jindal might never have hoisted upon us any assignments. She was generous with her grading and mild with her punishments, never treating one student any different from another. However, I was soon beginning to realise that she set me apart. Each time I submitted my notebook to her, she always looked at it a little queerly, first at the pages and then at my face. I might not have worried if she did not suggest one

Monday that a meeting be arranged with my parents. I nodded but reported no such thing at home. That only served to reveal a new side to Mrs Jindal: persistence. A month later, a letter arrived from school and Ma opened it so quickly, it nearly tore into two pieces. She probably expected me to have been expelled or sentenced to the gallows.

'What have you been doing at school?' Ma glared at me.

'What does the letter say?' I asked with genuine curiosity.

'Nothing,' she looked as puzzled, 'just that your class teacher wants to discuss your performance at school.'

And there I was, sitting equi-distant from Ma and Mrs Jindal, finding out that I had no writing unique to my hand. Ma's fingers were lightly massaging her forehead where a little green vein throbbed. I knew that vein very intimately. It was the one that triggered the cane.

Mrs Jindal was saying, 'I wish I knew where the problem lies. This is Aditi's notebook. Please have a look at it. It is as if each essay were written by a different person. For a while I actually wondered if that was the case, but now it is becoming clear to me that the child does not have really have handwriting of her own.'

I was able to see where Mrs Jindal's distress was coming from. I wrote only because I had been told that I had to. It was not my fault that the alphabets rebelled, that they hated me and each other. They also hated to become words or phrases or sentences or to be put together in any order, which usually left me with little more than a scrawl.

'Every page in her notebook is written in a different hand,' Mrs Jindal was saying. That was true: some letters lying low in deference, some cockily propped upright, some looped like a circus trick. 'Sometimes she even writes each sentence in a different hand.' That too was difficult to deny. Often I had tried to amuse myself by writing like this person or that, usually whoever sat next to me in class, but no matter how hard I tried, I could not write like myself. 'I think we should give her some writing exercises, so that she can start again from the alphabets,' Mrs Jindal kindly suggested to Ma whose throbbing vein had by now turned a deep purple.

To slip back to A-B-Cs when nearly in my teens? It was a preposterous thought. I looked at Ma and shifted in my chair. Knowing how temperamental she could be, I was prepared to bolt if need arose.

'Is this all you want to discuss with me?' Ma finally sighed. I knew I was safe. She did not think the matter merited any fuss.

'Yes,' said the brave Mrs Jindal and then after a pause, 'from my experience as a teacher, I can suggest that this is often never really about the handwriting. The child may have some self-esteem problems...at home perhaps...'

'Is it about the handwriting or is it not?' Ma's voice became sharp.

Mrs Jindal could only nod now. The meeting was over.

Ma stood up and said, 'Well, give her writing exercises each day. I will make sure she does it. The writing should form itself soon'. It did not. Not as easily as Ma had made it out to be.

I was condemned to spend many months with a special notebook meant to reform the offending alphabets. Four lines, parallel to each other. The two red lines in the centre running inside two blue ones were the bulwark where all the small letters had to be fitted in. The capital letters and those that looped above had to touch the first line. For those loops that tailed below the alphabet, I would have to drag my pen as low as the last blue line. Worse, every single alphabet after being so monstrously stretched between lines, had to be connected to each other into a word. Row after row, page after page – and then to repeat the feat on a blank sheet without the safety net of the guiding lines.

For a child on the verge of forfeiting her sense of self, the loss of any identifiable handwriting is negligible. Yet she tries to be seek that elusive consistency in her lettering. She tries till Mrs Jindal gives up and settles for the first legible pattern. Or she tries till Ma suggests it would be better to learn typing. Either way, she tries and fails.

29

A RAINY MORNING HAS DRENCHED THE HOUSE. MARIA IS closing the backdoor softly as she slips out into the rain under her orange cover. There are three holes in that umbrella, the reason why Ma decided that Maria could have it. Three spots of light. Maria walks in the rain taking great care to keep the leaky holes away from her white cotton dress. The rain is talking, in a steady rhythmic whisper, to the window panes, to the leaves, to the agitated puddles, to the roof, to the brave orange umbrella. Maria is swallowed by the downpour as I watch from my bed by the window.

That same evening, it is still raining. The house is crowded with people, the little corner near the door piled with drippy umbrellas, the floor smudged by the mud from their shoes and the dining table – the dining table! – loaded like we had never seen it before. Its wooden legs almost creaking with ecstasy, plain white cutlery hidden under a burst of colours: the rich brown of the mutton curry, the green of the watery spinach, the profusion of cottage cheese in golden paste, the speckled yellow rice and the rainbows in the pastries.

We have been carefully dressed for the evening. The brothers are wearing identical shirts in blue. I am in that hateful pink polka dotted frock, still too small for it. We are all standing in a line near the wall, me so close to the curtains that I snuggle a little under its folds for the comfort of invisibility. Ma has told us to behave ourselves. Afraid to move or breathe too loudly, we gape at the sarees and trousers that shuffle around the room, some stopping by to sprinkle a few pleasantries around us. Maria has changed from the white dress into a dark green saree acquired from our dead grandmother's sparse wardrobe. She is carrying around a tray with glasses, conscious of the many eyes that linger on her slender waist and the rounded flesh that peeks above the drape of the fabric on her chest.

It is the only party I remember being held in our house, even if the reason and recollection of the celebrations has now been rendered hazy, because of something incredible which happened at that instant.

Ma walks into the room.

She is wearing a light pink chiffon saree and her dark hair has loosened from its customary low knot to plunge down to her waist. On Ma's left shoulder, pinning her saree to her blouse, is a dazzling golden insect. She wears no other jewellery and this one seemed to wear her on itself. A dragonfly pin. Why had I never seen it before? Where did it come from? My eyes do not leave Ma, do not blink nor waver, till we are lead out of the room by Maria.

It is an apparition that mystifies the senses: carelessly lyrical and more beautiful than the frailest gossamer, the dragonfly sucks out every beam of brightness from creation to flash into my depths.

The visitors compliment Ma on the saree, the food, the furniture, the quiet children, the liveliness, even the weather that she had nothing to do with. I wait eagerly for someone to ask her about the dragonfly. Nobody does so. It is too exasperating. And all this while, the dragonfly continues to stare back at me. The eyes, red rubies, are glowing coals in the golden sheen of its head: its glassy vitreous wings and fragile body suggests it has alighted perchance on Ma to rest briefly before taking flight again. I cling to the curtains to suppress the desire to run over to Ma and touch her shoulder. Maria comes around to persuade us to retire to our rooms for dinner. I try to stall but am pulled out.

Ma turns to the light and the creature twinkles with her. Precocious. Another child born and raised unknown to us, nestled on her breast, nude and tantalising, my sibling the dragonfly. She laughs and the silence on her shoulder turns volatile; dizzying spaces between her feet and earth; a storm between its wings and the emptying room. She looks around and they dissolve together. Pallid gold spreads finely among the silhouettes. She is swaying at the edge of the precipice where outrageous desires are born and I'm willing to fall.

Sleep vanishes that night. The dragonfly pin, I tell myself, must be the most exquisite thing in the world! Where did Ma get it from? Would she mind if I had just one good look at it? Surely not. Maybe I can still find it by her mirror or in her drawer and hold it in my palms. I only want a few minutes alone with it. Just one look.

I am out of bed and walking in the dark before a second thought can deter me. I open the door but don't get any further. Sitting on the stairs is Ma, her back to my door. Her light pink saree has paled into a dull cream in the little light of a distant table lamp. I begin to gently close the door when something is said. I pause. Maasi is speaking. I step ahead to have a better look. The drawing room is empty but corners of it still hold traces of the crowded chaotic evening.

'It will only take us a few more minutes of work. Let's clean it all up.'

'No Meeta. I'm exhausted! Maria will do it in the morning. I wish I could sleep but I am too tired for that too!'

'Why today?'

'What do you mean?'

'You know what I mean! The dragonfly, of course! Why did you have to wear the brooch today? How can you ever wear it? I don't understand you…'

My ears tremble. What about the dragonfly?

'What are you holding on to? Why don't you just return it? Or give it to some charity? Or just put it in some bank locker so that we will never have to look at it again? Have you kept the rest of them also at home?'

The rest? I am overwhelmed by the implication that there are more like the dragonfly. And was Maasi out of her mind to speak so spitefully of something so spectacular? What does Ma have to say?

Ma does not say anything. Her delicate neck hangs low, the hair pulled back in its bundled severity. She looks entombed. A big invisible spear is running diagonal through her left shoulder, piercing her heart and pinning her down to the wooden board of the stairs.

30

WE NEVER SAW THE DRAGONFLY AGAIN. I TRIED TO ASK MA about it but she brushed me aside. I began to search through her cupboard and dresser out of a desperate need to make sure it had not just been a delusion. Ma caught me out. Initially I feigned confusion. Soon I had no more excuses for being found with my hands buried till the elbows in her personal effects. The punishment could not be avoided.

The cane by then had acquired an exclusive taste of my skin. The boys had accepted all of Ma's rules that needed abiding but not me. I continued to look for the dragonfly.

One would imagine that being caned for most of the young life would teach skin cells to be indifferent or the mind to create a pretence of feeling no pain. That is ridiculously untrue. Every caning hits the skin as much as the essence of life beneath. It falls, a shattering thunderbolt in gaudy daylight. It lunges upward like the tidal surf. It seeps, perishes like dew that drops on the desert dunes. The pain and humiliation never dim nor does its memory ever retreat. That memory then gives birth to another, and together they make a third. Memories of the cane and the skin and the shame.

The bruises stay on to become scars. The scars then dry up on the skin. And the memories spawn till there is space for neither cane nor skin nor shame.

the artist

31

STAYING IN THE HILLS WHEN THE WINTER AMBUSHES THE
sun and there is barely any certainty that life will sustain, one
learns to count on the inescapable: frost, heavy rolling mists and
winds like sharpened icicles that persistently pierce the body.
The cold hurries to camp in as early as possible and stays on
till the summer warmth emerges to suppress it to being just a
nip in the night air. A new entity has moved into my room since
the blacksmith's daughter left to chase her ghosts – Time. It
sits in the many corners and lines of the little room and around
my lone bed. Shadows grow ominous by the minute. They prey
on the heart. Blood in the veins grows sluggish, often freezes.
The windows are rarely opened. All around, books lay forgotten
but not too dusty, for Time sometimes uses them as a seat to
gloat at me from. In a corner, a puny room heater grudgingly
gives warmth to both of us.

The Big House is doing lean business, or so it seems. The
battalion led by the Great Sister has dwindled but a few white
uniforms are still clicking their heels with persistence. They nag,
taunt and coax me through various routines including walks in
the bare frosty garden and eating in the dining hall. I'm too cold
to protest. The garden strolls are particularly distasteful because

Time runs around me in expanding circles, sometimes swishing past and sometimes mockingly trailing my footsteps. I try ducking into the bushes or sitting down on a bench, as still as the stone sculpture nearby, but Time always catches up.

Eventually I begin to look forward to the trips to the dining hall. Time stays back in the room to sulk while I am free to relax and laugh at my housemates. Each person is on a different diet and no two meals look alike. The three stern ladies who bring in the plates don't bother to stay back to discuss the finer aspects of the cuisine or make polite talk. I am desultorily light-headed, free of my haunting companion, studying plates and matching the contents to possible ailments their diners suffer from; all of which requires vast and shrewd guesswork.

'Carrots are the most miserable of all vegetables,' says the fat man at the far end of the table. His fork fiddles with a boiled carrot stick, a cat with a dead mouse who is suddenly and uncharacteristically disgusted to be eating putrid flesh instead of white creamy milk. He may not want to consider it now but the constipated ones who scoff at their fibres are heading for infernal trouble. I pity him a little.

'I don't think I will agree with you,' says the shrill school-teacher from a nearby town, who has been dropped at the Big House by her husband for another 'much deserved vacation'. Every morning she looks worse off than the previous day, her short hair falling off in patches. From certain angles she looks bald. Even the bright scarf around her neck does not distract enough from the pocked and blotchy skin. I guess her to be twenty years younger than her appearance; her voice, pitchy and firm from shouting at devilish students. It is a voice that can give gruff generals a fright on the battlefield. Sadly full of life. Ebbing life.

'The murky soup should talk!' mutters the auntie who lives directly below my room. She now sit at my right elbow and fortunately has not been heard by the school-teacher.

'Carrots…beetroots…and what is that other fat round vegetable that grows on a vine?' The fat man has paid little attention to all that has been said since his last comment, but we nod our heads in gratitude for having started a conversation that everyone with a tongue to spare can add a word or two.

'Pumpkin?' the teacher slurps on her soup but looks up with the information.

'No…no…' the fat man is not satisfied.

'Only cows eat grass. If I don't get meat to eat, I might consider cooking one of you,' threatens the brooding young man who reads the same book each day at dinner. He claims it is an awful book but since the food is equally unappetising, it helps him tide through both.

'Cancer, unfortunately, does not write a menu card after consulting you.' The auntie-below can be habitually mean and difficult to shut. She gives me indigestion as well as cramps in the right arm which has begun to battle with the food. For some insane reason, each time I brave the dining room she refuses to sit anywhere but an inch from me. I may have more luck shaking a bloodhound off my tracks.

'Cancer? Who has cancer?' says the young man looking up sharply towards us. My neighbour clatters her fork into an empty plate and belches loudly. I am becoming resolute about throwing something hard at the floor later in the night to give her a ringing headache. She has ruined my appetite. I look down intently at a little brown chunk in the gravy. If meat, it can be offered to the young man who has bent his head further into the fading book, a little startled by his own sudden outrage. Nobody has reacted to the question though the answer is known to all.

The fat man suddenly blurts out, 'Yes, the pumpkin! If I meet anybody growing pumpkins, I will have a few serious things to say to that person!'

'Much like the drumstick. To be chewed on only to be spat out. Why bother to chew at all? I like to eat something I can swallow.' This is the lady who sits next to the book-reading young man.

Most of us never bother with names and introductions. We know each other from our place at the table and the food in our plates. The lady with the drumstick aversion always dresses immaculately, sits upright at the table, holds her cutlery with pride and elegantly chews every morsel. I think she chooses to sit next to the young man because he appears to be the only sign of intellect in a carnival of boors. I think, for the same reason, the auntie-below sits with me. She finds me suitably coarse for her company. I will not disappoint her. I push my chair back and the plate forward on the table, a trifle disdainfully. The drumstick lady winces at the screechy sounds.

'The greatest aspiration of man on the social level is the sacred freedom to live without the need to work,' the young man reads aloud, his nose deeply wedged between the pages. I nod my approval.

There was a time the dining hall used to be full of people, most of them pleasant, but those were also the days I stayed in my room, battling for my right over the blanket with the Great Sister. It was only when Time imposed itself continuously on me that I was forced to consider communal dining.

'But carrots...' the fat man's voice cracks. He is running out of reasons to stall the meal. Hunger must sit in his room the same as Time does in mine, the carrots as much on his mind as on his plate. My pity deepens.

'Oh, shut up and eat!' says the school-teacher. She pushes her bowl aside. The lines of pain have spread from her face to the veins in her wrist. I stifle a great impulse to touch her; as if she senses that, she gets up, nods her head stiffly at nobody in particular and shimmers out of the room.

'Did you hear about the twins? Terrible news!' whispers the woman at my elbow and I jump a little. Although the other eyes at the table are still on their plates, their ears have turned to us now.

'Really?' It is the most reserved response I could present at such short notice. Same as the others, I have come to expect nothing more drastic from the twins but a routine and a periodic physical growth that they suffer in unison.

'Sure. The head-nurse loves to drop in and chit-chat every now and then. She told me so herself.' The woman picks her teeth, holds out a little piece of green to the light and carefully places it on her tongue to prevent it from getting caught again.

I am bursting from the need to know more, but having established my credentials in this company almost entirely by being non-committal and disinterested in everything including the food, I am reluctant to make a departure. To descend to their ranks is to throw myself at the mercy of hyenas with a bad sense of humour. I bite my tongue and quickly swallow a glass of water in regret. That does not go unnoticed and a few glances are exchanged.

The auntie-below shrugs, 'If you promise not to ever drop anything on the floor and on my head, I might tell you'. She has a twisted mind, this woman. And to add to that, the terrible company she keeps for small talk – the mental picture of her and the Great Sister sharing an evening of gossip churns my stomach. I keep my peace, unwilling to make any rash promise for a little information that won't radically change my life.

The conversation on vegetables resumes. A lot of enthusiasm is beginning to build on the importance of rubbing the right amount of salt for the right number of minutes into the spine of an obstinate bitter-gourd to make it lose its character.

'We are having nice weather indeed,' I mutter and sit back to pretend being marooned on an island with nothing but miles of blue salt water to gaze at and only one last glass of sweet drinkable water for company. A little gust of hot breath brushes over my nape. Time, I realise, is standing right behind me.

I AM DRAWN TO THEIR ROOM ALMOST AGAINST MY WILL, A temptation I cannot resist having never seen it empty before. Religious morality has frequently assailed my heart but I have never opened my doors to it, not even when Nani had threatened a possible rebirth in a pig sty. It helped my cause that the parents believed in the university-god and none other. I have often wandered into temples and churches of the neighbourhood when they were certain to be deserted. No, not to pray but to stand there and breathe the air of solitude, of a calm seasoned into vintage by little icons of devotion. Being in the twins' room reminds me of that bliss.

I walk around as slowly as I can. It is an art gallery like no other. No frames to constrain the colours; the figures free to run from one wall to another or from the floor to the ceiling. I stand in rapt attention to the inconspicuous corners behind windows that pulsate with a distinct motif. For the little details drawn at the base of the walls, I have to lie down flat on my stomach. Once satisfied with a thorough perusal, I jump on the table to study the birds painted on scrawny trees higher up. Then I see, that the birds are actually cats. How curious that I have never noticed that before! The trees are full of cats, not a single bird or anything remotely winged. The fur on one of the cats vaguely resembles feathers as the cat starts to jump off a bough and heads towards one of the dozens of suns embossed on the walls.

After a while, I do manage to locate a few birds where they are busy scavenging in the thick undergrowth. I crouch low again. Against the same backdrop emerge an assortment of animals, resplendent in a patchwork of colours, with not even the remotest resemblance between any two of them. Each gleaming pair of eyes is the lone representative of a nameless species. A couple of them insolently watch the cats in the trees. I am nearly delirious. Here is something that grabs the soul and forces joy down its throat!

Why did we as children all attempt the same sort of drawings – mountain peaks born of one undulating line, thatched huts or buildings with minimal ventilation, curly-headed trees on shaky feet, round suns pierced with sticks pointing in all directions? The twins, with their discovery that the world can be re-invented in its representation, had everyone fretting about their unnatural obsession.

I watch the walls till the traces of their labour – dabs, strokes, dribbles, smudges, layers, flecks, sprays, streaks, blobs, shades – spin around me in mad abandon. I lurch towards the door, forcefully evicting my limbs, not wanting to be discovered here by the twins in their absence. It might be construed as a desecration of their space. My admiration is tainted. What could I possibly offer their art but lustful and envious gazing?

33

HE HAD BEEN CHOSEN FROM AMONG THOUSANDS OF BOYS who gathered for prayers at the ashram each day. He stood the same as them, in perfectly aligned rows, with folded palms and eyes squeezed shut. He did not understand any of the chants they had to repeat loudly. All he wanted was to go out to the fields, swing from tamarind trees, swim in the cool streams and lie in the shadow of his mother's lap listening to her broken tunes. And yet, he was destined to be picked for a life that was not his own.

Born alongside six children both older and younger than him, all fitted into a small two-roomed tin-roofed house with a pessimistic father and a mother pregnant with the eighth, he never grudged the constant hunger, the endless quarrels among the children, the apathy of his father, the despair of his mother, the crumbling walls or the leaking roofs. Instead he was filled with a deep joy of living: admiring the seasons, longing for the moon, loving puppies tumbling down the streets and happiest when he missed school. After three years of failing to clear the elementary grade, his father saw the futility of spending money on his education and ordered that he go to the ashram instead. So he stood happily with the poorest of the neighbourhood, said the prayers they expected him to, accepted the role of the community dunce and continued to be filled with joyfulness. However he was easily noticed in his detachment and the man in charge of the boys spoke to one of the senior teachers. The word spread fast among the teachers and soon reached the ears of the great guru.

The boy was summoned to the dark inner chambers where intense penance was said to be carried out, a holy place not exposed to common eyes, suffused with incense and soaked in the light of oil lamps. The guru held the boy in his arms, closed his eyes and meditated for ten minutes. The boy, deeply inhaling the sandal perfume and soaking the gentle warmth of the man's bare skin, fell asleep.

He dreamt of rainbows that flowed on earth as rivers. Something was compelling him to lunge into those swirling patterns. He saw his own body fall towards one blending shade and then another. The waters closed over his head but did not wet him. Inside the river of colours was pitch darkness.

He woke up to find himself sleeping in the softest bed. It brought a surge of sensation as never before, the silk sheets and the cool breeze brushing over his skin. Unable to withstand the peculiar comfort, he awoke crying. A group of men stood around him and watched reverentially.

The guru announced that he had seen the rarest gilded vacuum inside the boy, a sign of sure greatness. He sent for the boy's parents and talked to them for hours in a shut room. The father morosely declared that he had no objections to anything the great man wanted to do with his rather dim-witted son. The mother cried for the loss but thanked the gods for blessing her womb so generously. They both agreed to hand over their son's upbringing over to the ashram trust and severe all ties with him. The boy was allowed to meet them for one last time. He did not understand their explanations for deserting him or the distance that everyone kept as their heads bowed low to him. He sought answers but none came his way. All that the guru was willing to say was that this special boy would be prepared for his future as a man of great wisdom and spiritual light.

The chosen boy grew older in the protective shade of the ashram. No attempts were made to teach him anything or interfere with his natural impulse. Only a small group of people were allowed to talk to him. He was never to venture beyond the ashram gates or miss the guru's discourse in the evenings. He slept on silk sheets but was not to be touched, either by his former playmates or by his caregivers.

Devotees visiting the ashram knew of the existence of such a young visionary who they would have to follow and obey someday but since the guru would not allow it till his own death, they hesitated to get too close to the boy, in distance or in familiarity.

He was a handsome and willowy twenty-two year old when the guru turned cold. The doors of the ashram were thrown open the following day. Everyone came to see the successor, including the boy's parents who sat quietly in the crowds where nobody recognised them. They had come not to see their son, but the promised preacher.

The young man of such promise walked out of the inner chambers, saw the sea of expectant faces, turned to the tall door that opened to daylight and began to walk out. Around him, the voices of his superiors reverentially tried to restrain him and devotees whispered for blessings. He continued to walk, out of the hall, through the gate, into the fields and away from the ashram. He had nothing to teach them.

For a while he loitered around in the streets. Lost. The world appeared to him to have been transformed into a different entity during the many years he had been shut away. Where would he go? What would he do for his next meal? He wandered down the lane of his childhood home. It was almost unrecognisable.

A discoloured and irregular room had grown attached to it like an abscess. The walls had been fortified with bricks in some places, moving the front door to a different side. Only the window looked familiar and he greedily peered in. He saw four boys playing inside, all strangers who were born to his mother. There was no place for him there. He walked away and never looked back.

Nobody heard from him ever again. Ten years later, somebody in the ashram saw a man in the newspaper who looked familiar despite the cover of a thick beard. The writing below was about an Indian artist in Paris who had dazzled the contemporary art circles with an original and striking collection. One of the men hurriedly fetched a magnifying lens and the picture was carefully studied. The face almost resembled the boy who had walked away from his duty of saving souls, but there was no way to be sure. It was difficult to explain how a boy who had no survival skills or the means to any livelihood had become an artist of such international repute. The lens was put away with the newspaper and the men agreed that they were looking at the face of a different person. Their lost guru, they believed, had embarked on a pilgrimage of the world and would return to them someday.

Vishnu was that man in the picture. He was also the boy who had wandered into the throngs of men without a past or a future. As for the years in between, it would remain a mystery. He never sought publicity, avoided social gatherings and let only his paintings speak to the world. During exhibitions, his enigmatic smile was the perfect cover, almost hypnotising buyers who stood weakened by his creative powers and did not worry about the price of a work they felt compelled to take home. In the art fraternity, for the few who got close to him, Vishnu was as much a philosopher as an artist. He was articulate and rational. He believed that everything could be explained by the power of perception. He rarely spoke of god and argued that great art could be born only when an artist believed the highest power to rest within the human heart and not some celestial sphere.

Vishnu's commitment to his work was legendary. He laboured on his studies and concepts, compromising with nothing but his own health and space. At the age of forty, he had been acknowledged as the most innovative and dynamic artist of his times. A little into his fifties, Vishnu found out, quite by accident, that he had fathered a son from a passionate encounter with a woman he barely knew. He was neither overjoyed nor confused. He spoke to the boy's mother and offered to generously support them so long as they did not expect his physical attendance. She gladly took the offer and they never met again.

His paintings, constantly being picked up by discerning art collectors, were beginning to get auctioned at prestigious galleries. The monetary rewards were becoming almost as high as his reputation. Now in his sixties, Vishnu was aghast at how suffocating art could become when it was made to tarry with business. He decided not to hold any more exhibitions but send his work to one trusted art dealer who would then make sure they reached a small and select circle of patrons. He began to stay away from the cities, travelling into the countryside, staying with

strangers and changing names frequently. He lost himself yet
again in multitudes that did not care where he came from or the
definition of his art so long as he stayed quiet and nondescript.

<h1 style="text-align:center">34</h1>

THE AIR IS CHILLY ENOUGH FOR THE BLOOD TO CONGEAL
and yet the man who put this house up from its first brick did
not have the good sense to insulate it against cold or throw in
modest fireplaces for the rooms. Did he intentionally wish these
walls to be unkind? Later, from one of the many dining hall talks,
I gathered that it was a woman's hand that had designed this
place, a minimalist whose buildings were economical to
construct – which explains how she got the job – but formidable
in every manner possible. She had built a house that had the
potential to be a furnace in summer and a giant ice cube in
winter. Most times during the day, it is colder indoors than if
one had to be out in the open, braving the mountain gales.

Time, unwelcome visitor, has grown lazier since: putting on
weight, growing bulky, sitting in my room for hours, days,
weeks. We are mutually uncomfortable with meeting each
other's gaze. From my window I am able to see a little crowd
gathering on the lawns to soak up the little sunlight spreading
itself thin this morning. Hesitation, if any, is fleeting. I look for
the walking shoes.

'I never though the twins capable of it. It is…it is…
unimaginable!' says the fat man, cheerful when not confronted
with carrots.

Everyone knows the twins are gone, deducing that they had either tired of the place or the place had tired of them. I am definitely crushed for not having put in a few parting words. However, of what value are words to them? The paintbrushes I had borrowed are lying on my window-sill in a broken porcelain cup. They must have sneaked into my room to leave those behind for me. I will miss the twins but all scores have been matched and it is the best way for friends to part.

We all sit in a circle of wrought-iron, garden furniture painted greyish-white, squinting our eyes partly to cut out the glare from the sky and partly to avoid seeing too much of each other in the daylight. Without the dinner table between us, the ring of thought wavers and is sadly exposed. I perch myself first on the chair and then slip down on the grass instead. It is a bad decision. The grass is damp and soggy but having made a dramatic descent with exaggerated ease, there is no going back.

The young man with his favourite book sticks out a leg to drape over my empty chair while I continue to soak up the earth. 'I agree. It's certainly very scary. I visited their empty room early in the morning. Q-u-i-t-e terrible!' the book-man says, carefully turning a browning page. His fingers nimbly pull out the bookmark from the previous page and gently slip it into this one. He seems to know that everyone's eyes have been captured by his fingers which straighten unnaturally, attempting to be taller than they are. I am the first to look away and meet the gaze of the well-dressed lady, who by force of habit sits near him. Today she is wearing a large ring on her finger, a circle of blue stone embedded in silver.

'Why would do they do something so strange just before leaving?' she is looking straight into my eyes.

The auntie-below decides to speak instead. 'They... were...ill...' she says, enunciating each word carefully so that her actual thoughts don't elude us – they had lost their marbles.

I don't want her to say any more and let my loyalties be known. 'They were wonderful. I wish they had stayed on.'

'Everyone wants to leave. Don't you want to go back home too?'

'Home?'

'Home, to your brothers. You are lucky to have them, you know. They visit you so often...'

'That is because I am not a relationship they had to earn or nurture. I was always there, part of the package, like an accessory that comes cheap or even free with a gadget you buy.'

'What an unkind thing to say!'

And then the words just slip out of me, 'I was there last night.'

'Where?'

'In their room. I watched them but they did not notice me. They were busy...'

'The twins? And what happened then?'

I open my mouth to speak. Some experiences are private. Too private. I swallow the words resolutely.

'Well? Tell us!' they all wait for me to betray my old friends.

'You should read this book. I can lend it to you if you want me to,' says the young man, feeling sorry for me.

I ignore him. Something at a little distance is drawing my attention. Time is out in the garden with the rest of us, peering at the little bush which once carried white blooms. Voices resound and fade around me but I cannot hear them. Time is walking around the bush, round and round till I feel dizzy. I get up quickly and hurry over. Time looks down where a small banished plastic bottle lies half-buried. It looks forlorn. I kick some mud loose with my shoes, shove the bottle in and use both feet to quickly smother it down. Time shakes his head at me sadly. I continue to stamp over the new grave defiantly.

Someone is calling my name. The crowd is heading back towards the building. A fleet of clouds are gathering fast over our heads, tossed dangerously by strong blasts of the cold wind. I am shifting my body weight ever so slightly between the two feet to keep the blood circulating. And although my spirit is racing in my veins, galvanised into action like it hasn't for years, my body being used to sloth, hesitates.

'What am I doing here?' I ask a rare question; rare, because I have never ever questioned anything that comes my way.

Time shrugs in reply and looks through me. I turn away instinctively. The Big House looks grotesque. Its geometric forms long admired for an 'elegant countryside look' is now a dark frown on the landscape, the fog rapidly engulfing it. I begin walking towards it, slowly and resolutely, and then involuntarily turn around. The bush is still there but Time is gone. I know I will have to leave too.

A large bubble floats in from the distant peaks, hovers above my head and sucks me to the centre of its transparent cavity. I let it.

the errant heart

35

THERE IS NO SUCH THING AS 'FROM THE HEART', PA OFTEN said.

Ma agreed with him: all decisions are taken by the head, though some may be less thought through. The heart is only an organ pumping blood.

Only an organ.

Descriptions like this may seem dry and brittle enough to crumble but they stay with a child. They certainly stuck with the four of us. The brothers treated all women with courteous indifference. During their teenage years, when their friends slashed wrists for gawky girls or copied romantic poetry from the college library, Ma's sons stayed true to her teachings.

Amar, being the eldest, was often made fun of. Whether he was ploughing the trail for the three of us, it is hard to say. The girls apparently found his stodgy sanity very attractive and constantly flirted, asking for class notes, advice on personal dilemmas and even shy requests to share coffees with them. He was polite but aloof with all of them, an attitude that drove the other boys crazy. Being ignored did the same to the girls.

'Is it true that you prefer boys to girls?' he was asked more than once, for who in their right mind would refuse unconditional adulation from the opposite sex?

'I prefer intelligent people,' he would reply with a straight face.

The peers gave up, it being no fun to mock those who react with such severe sobriety. When Arun landed in the same college, it surprised them that there was another like the first but the brothers stuck together. Having spent a lot of time in a common room, sharing everything from study tables to deodorants, it was easy for them to meet and chat in-between classes. At the start of the following year, Anand joined to complete the old combination. They had individual idiosyncrasies, but the bonding was unmistakable; so also the inclination to stay away from fun – girls, parties and all the rebellion the rest were frolicking in. Ma had worked just too assiduously for any transitory external influences to reverse.

Pa did not give their peculiarities much thought: 'Nature will take its course. They cannot always sustain off each other.'

Ma insisted: 'Marriage is a compromise. My children will be intellectually free and happy in their differences. They don't need someone else to feel complete.'

Laila, unlike Maria, was not afraid to voice her opinion: 'The boys will make great husbands and any woman will be lucky to have them. But who will marry the girl?'

The brothers are all still single, living together with no signs of ever contributing to the propagation of the species. Need I say more?

Is it compulsory for memories to come accompanied by emotions? Maybe we pick one from a basket of many because it evokes something – pain, joy, sorrow, nostalgia, regret, longing, contentment. Most of the ones that interest me now are those that mean nothing, which brings me to the next thought – the whitewash of memories. Facts become distorted by our prejudices, our longings and failings when we live them; and then, as the events dry up to become memories, like grapes into raisins, there is nothing left of the original but our ability to extract its essence. Sometimes, we drop a memory along the way. How much baggage can a person ultimately haul? Sometimes, the memory transforms itself back into an experience. Often, something worse happens. A new memory grows over the previous one until it completely takes over that space. The whitewash. If the previous memory was more precious, then the mind suffers great loss. If the new memory, now safely latched on to the rest of the remembrances is a beautiful one, there still remains a sense of loss because what is this can never really be that. The older memory, which then lies forgotten under the new coat of paint, can never be reclaimed.

Did both Pa and Ma lose their minds, their spirits, at the same time? Were we all swept away in that cumulative frustration from being numbed to those unknown possibilities of existence that one has to risk and the madness that makes life real? I ask all of it now. Sitting here at the foot of towering mounds of earth, allowing everyone to believe that I do not act because I dare not think, I have learnt to keep my secrets well.

36

LAILA WAS AN ABLE REPLACEMENT TO MARIA WHEN SHE LEFT with her stomach of woes. It brought about a new regime. The beefy wife of our neighbourhood washerman, Laila had ten children of her own and treated us like the troops that Ma had envisioned. No more of Maria's gentle cooing and persuasions. Laila made us dread her active fierce tongue and the fleshy arms that swung around dangerously close to our heads. Ma was thrilled with her find. I might have suffered greatly in Laila's care if fortune had not been kind enough to arrange a propitious meeting.

Nandita was one of those prodigies that all mothers compulsively love: an intelligent, articulate girl who, soon after she learnt to walk steadily, got busy winning prizes and accolades. She was the only child of her parents, so repeatedly described as 'brilliant' that everyone seemed to wait for her to literally clamber on top of some great peak and wave a flag. We studied in different schools but met occasionally in the neighbourhood, both of us having ample reason to hold the other in disdain. And yet we would soon be inseparable.

Laila did not stay in our house. She went back to her own brood every night, who unlike the young of the moneyed, were accustomed to looking after themselves. She watched me with dark suspicious eyes, an open dislike that I managed to reflect right back at her. The brothers with their penchant for flourishing under dominating women were treated like princes. I did my best to keep away from all of them.

I found a friend in Nandita whose parents are probably never going to forgive me for the bad influence I was on their little genius. It was obvious that her new-found love for loitering on the streets could be attributed to me, but she was a rather satisfactory single child and I was tolerated, much like a wart on an angel.

Laila struck me only once and Nandita made sure she never touched me again.

We had decided to bake a cake from a recipe excavated from one of the novels that Nandita was reading. She said, 'See, writers ought to write like this! Who cares if the English heroine managed to make something edible enough for her French lover? The writer had the good sense to make sure there was a believable cake at the end of it.'

I cared not for the book or the romance but the idea of a cake was delectable even if it had to be executed in Ma's kitchen since the three eggs so poetically described by the admirable writer would be a scandal in Nandita's brahmin household. We waited for the perfect baking day and an empty house while Nandita finished reading the same book twice – apparently the French lover who loved the cake more than the cook appealed to her imagination – and carefully copied the recipe on a long sheet of paper with notes in the margin so that there would be no ambiguity on each of our roles. She was to measure and my ungainly arms were deemed suitable for the mixing.

Our baking day arrived when both Pa and Ma disappeared without telling each other or any of us where they intended to be. They had begun doing that often enough for us to be sure that neither would turn up before sundown. Anand had the flu and strict orders to stay in bed. Amar took one peek at us in the kitchen and walked out with Arun in tow, deciding to be safely away at the library before disaster or Ma struck. I had forgotten all about Laila who had been sent on the weekly grocery shopping. It was too late to think of a plan to avoid her when she turned up at the doorway and surveyed the battlefield that the dough, eggs, sugar and butter had turned the kitchen into. Nandita was standing on a chair, a marble statuette covered in flour that I had sprinkled in good humour, laughing at me while I dipped my head into the batter bowl to lick it clean.

Laila marched straight towards us, grabbed my collar and slapped as hard as she could when my bewildered face looked up from the bowl. Through the tears of pain that clouded my eyes, I saw the most unexpected spectacle. Nandita jumped right beside me and swung a big wooden spatula straight at Laila's head. Before the duel went any further, I grabbed Nandita's hands and dragged her behind me, running as fast as I could into the open. Laila screamed as we raced away from the house but Nandita was gleeful at her own audacity. I tried not to think of the horrors that would await me on returning home. My cheeks were flaming red and stinging with clear imprints of each of Laila's fingers but I did not care. I had found a hero.

37

I DID NOT BELIEVE THE DAY WOULD EVER COME WHEN THE campus house would have to be finally vacated. It is time – Ma declared – to own a roof that will outlast the trauma of retirement, abandonment by children, anonymity and old age penury. Pa spoke to a property broker, or rather was spoken to; a few houses were looked at and finally one purchased a little below market rates because of the architect's scant regard for vaastu. While most buyers had refused to live in a house that did not honour the path of the sun or the ancient laws of spatial alignment, my parents grabbed the opportunity to deviate from convention.

The new house was in a colony situated right outside the university walls. Till their deaths, both parents refused to accept that survival anywhere else would be just as easeful. That is the house where the dog now lives with the surviving men of the family.

A year after moving into the new house, the reluctant honour of being the only child at home was thrust upon me. The boys had packed and left for the hostel and the realisation hit Ma only when Anand waved a cheery goodbye. She had desperately wanted her sons to stay at home while they pursued higher studies and had said 'No student can hope for a house closer to the university than this. How convenient!'

Pa would not hear of it and ignored the boys' long faces because they sort of liked it there in Ma's shadow. For once he yelled louder than her, 'Let them go! It is the least I can do for them. Let them live on their own and become men. You cannot hide them forever under the drapes of your saree.'

Debates not being encouraged, they were categorically told that under no circumstances, unless they were dying or in jail, were they to call or come home during weekdays. It was their lot to pretend we lived in a remote country and face life like the others trapped in their hostel rooms. For a while, even the weekend trips were under a cloud because Pa thought a monthly visitation to be fair enough and Ma had to fight hard to restore that privilege. On the other six days, it became entirely my lot to represent the children of the household. I could not wait to leave home too and join a distant college: greater the distance, the dream uplifted itself to being a source of ecstasy. Those were to be my last days tied to the parental tether.

Ma panicked. I stayed indifferent. Pa told her to stop crying and stick her chin out. More than the absence of the boys, having to be a full-time mother to me began to wear her out. She aged by the hour. Her knees began to ache and the doctors said arthritis. Her stomach hurt and he suggested that she needed a hysterectomy. Her tooth ached and a couple of root canals were urgently recommended. The boys hovered in the proximity of the house like anxious bees.

Pa gave up trying to gift independence to his sons; to also watch Ma waste away in her bed was too much for him to deal with. He said he had to complete his research in his lifetime and shut himself up in the study. It was to be path-breaking and revolutionary enough to make all the historians in the world sit up in their chairs or take their hats off or whatever it is historians do when they read something they have not read before.

Pa was on the tracks of a prosperous ancient society that had disappeared without a trace. He believed he knew where their settlement lay, where it used to be. Each time the work was said to near completion, some rare document invariably fell out of library shelves and he would shut himself up for the next few months trying to integrate new dimensions to papers already heavy with the dust of time. He wrote many letters to learned men and universities abroad, littering the study table with numerous drafts of proposals. 'I need to travel. I need more funds,' he would fret. Ma always read calmly while he paced. If he whined too much, she carefully folded the newspaper on the table and then just as neatly, did the same with her glasses. It was the only sign that she was applying immense self-restraint, not saying what she really thought of the whole matter. Pa's academic mission was sacred to him, much like the cows to his family back in the dust bowls. An honest criticism was unwelcome, even dreaded. He seemed to have reached a tacit understanding with his wife: she organised the family as she wished but held her tongue when his work was mentioned.

He did finish his research but it caused neither tide nor ripple and probably became a book that could forget itself in the library. Pa did get a few invitations to lecture on the topic so dear to him but the cordial interest he encountered was only a slight to the great excitement expected. A dream was what broke Pa's back. Ma had to finally request her sister to come and live with us till things got better. They never did.

Searching through my bundle of past images, I find many missing; causes and effects are fading with their treasure of details. I have to strain my ears to listen to snatches from the past and then repeat the voice of this one, very faintly and softly does it rise from within me. It was a Sunday and all the sons had turned up predictably enough from their hostels. Ma sat on a tall stool and supervised the puris that Laila kept bringing to the table.

The brothers were freshly washed, tucked in neatly ironed clothes, faces beaming from the gratitude of being under the homestead. They licked their fingers and looked adoringly at sweaty Laila as she dipped the puris in bubbling oil. The smoke rising thick from the stove moved away from the exhaust fan and stayed trapped in the room. Pa energetically strode towards the dining table and then stood aimlessly, twitching his wrists.

Ma raised an eyebrow at Laila. A fresh table mat and shiny steel plate appeared between our many elbows.

Pa sat down and began to talk, which surprised all of us because he usually could not muster energy to listen, 'The conference was very well organised. Prof. Modak kept telling everyone that my theory will put a question mark on...and the hotel was so very good despite...Pyarelal is getting ahead of himself in the catering business...what are you separating the peas from the potatoes for? They don't look poisonous to me... the students were so receptive, it was such a pleasant surprise...Amar! You better eat every single pea...difficult subject...and all the delegates began to laugh...' He talked as he ate, gaily, about this and that, making specific comments about us, remembering the days gone by and planning for immortality, all in the same breath.

We did not dare look at him. All four of us had finished eating but not knowing how to interrupt the outburst, we clung to the table. Our fingers strummed on the greasy plates till Laila confiscated them. So we made water rings on the table, silently comparing our glossy doodles. Ma was leaning hard over her elbows like she did when the strain of being ignored began to niggle. We knew the table edge would leave deep red grooves on her fair arms, like bangles branded in the skin. It greatly disturbed the brothers, this sign that the harmony between our parents was in doubt.

Pa disappeared into his study. We sighed in relief and scampered away. That night, the doctor, grave and gruff, came to our house. Ma took him into her bedroom, whispering to us, 'Be as quiet as you can. Pa is not feeling too well.'

'What is wrong with him?' I asked. She turned her face and briskly walked away.

The doctor did not look at any of us on his way in. He would usually pat my cheeks, a sign of recognition of my regular visits to his clinic through a childhood of injuries and fractures. That night, he was so grim, we felt like intruders in our own house. After he left Pa's room, Ma accompanied the doctor to the gate where they had a long conversation in the moonlight.

We opened all the windows and tried very hard to listen but it was nothing more than a pantomime – fatigue on Ma's face while the doctor wore a mask, wooden and unyielding. A few words fell into the wind, some on our ears, and yet nothing made sense.

I never saw Pa as optimistic or articulate ever again. He stayed in his room for many weeks and resigned from his job without consulting Ma. She made her angry views well known to us but never reproached him. Something must have gone terribly wrong, for he soon grew balder, bonier and unbearably silent. So diminished was Pa's presence in the house that when he died, it made little difference. We had to struggle to become aware of missing something important; there was once a father and he was gone for good.

38

FOR EVERY CHOICE WE MAKE, THERE IS ANOTHER POSSIBILITY that we reject or overlook; the truth about each of us does not lie in the path we walk but in the ones we reject or the ones we never become aware of. That was Ma's anthem while her mother shook a silent head in disagreement. Nani had her own stance – one needs to simply 'be' and that is all God expected from us; if any extra points had to be earned, one had to repeat a few of those obscure chants trapped in scriptures. She kept her sanity that way. In between their battle lines was me.

That summer I was to discover that the world is one big happy carousel. Everything was possibly in the wrong place, waiting to get to somewhere better. We are caught in the same whirl, spinning dreams, switching loves, severing losses and seeking freedom. Inside the security of the circle, the excitement of the pursuit and the assured return to the point of displacement, life was bullishly shuffling around; everything could indeed switch places and nothing would change.

Tedious childhood was thankfully almost over but the uneventful school life I had to maintain was straining the nerves. Being ordinary can be a lot of work. Maria was becoming disinterested in her duties and dragged her feet, one gloomy thought or the other chained to her heart. Ma failed to motivate her with those late-night discourses we often heard conducted in the kitchen and finally informed us that we were old enough to do things around the house. It meant chores and more boredom. I did manage to smuggle in my share of fun, inconsequential but irresistible fun. It started innocently enough, and peculiarly, with a book.

The parents had one thing they firmly agreed on – a family tradition of foisting the children with books for birthday presents. That year was no different when they woke me up with a thicker book than usual. It was bound in and smelt of leather. Ma claimed it was a collector's item and would be my companion for life. I was despondent. What was a girl expected to do with pages and pages that had no illustrations and mooned over four little women who were cheerfully poor while they waited for a father named after a month?

Nandita looked with yearning at the book and wondered aloud if she could read it before I did. She did not have to plead too much. I had been waiting with a plan. A few weeks ago, her mother had bought a football in the hope of luring Nandita to the outdoors and putting some colour into her pale cheeks. We exchanged the book with the football. It was as simple as that.

Initially I exchanged only books, those that belonged to me as well as others in the house. My reputation began to grow. The children of the colony agreed it was exciting, glad to part with books they had tired of or pick up the ones that promised a good read. I was in grave danger of becoming the local librarian: a fairly distasteful thought. The brothers too began keeping close tabs on their books having heard rumours of my swapping abilities from some unidentified sources. Just as the smuggling of books begun to show signs of being a burden, I quickly made some adjustments to the business plan.

Rummaging in my closet, I found a golden-mane doll that had not been played with for years and gave it away for a tiny sports car that was shiny blue on its three wheels. By the end of the week, the car was picked up by a little boy in thick glasses who could reel automobile model numbers faster than his alphabets. He had brought with him a tacky but sturdy model of the solar system that went to the school science exhibit as my handiwork. I duly got a certificate of participation that Pa beamed over while handing me a crisp ten rupee note to buy ice cream as reward.

I was now exchanging anything that could be spared in the house and the youngsters who came in hope of bargains knew that I would not turn my back on anything so long as it was not an outright losing deal. Often I ended up with stuff that I had no use for but which could be used to amuse myself or to palm off something I did not want. My room and its contents were altering constantly. Anand who shared space with me was so confused and irritated by my eccentricities that he soon moved in with the elder brothers who gladly took him in. I continued to shift everything around so that nobody noticed the additions – a pile of comic books under my cot one day, a frazzled one-eyed teddy bear atop the window pelmet on another. The thrill of the game was in clinching a good exchange without being nabbed at home. Sometimes I was even called to negotiate similar swaps between other kids, which I did gladly, if not for commission, then for some goodwill and publicity of my services.

Whenever I went out to play or cycle around our houses that stood neat as matchboxes along the road, there were glances of recognition, even respect. Though I was careful to never do business at school where surviving Sister Judith was a full-time challenge, I was very accessible on the campus, mostly while I hung around the playground. A few desperate clients even dared make phone calls which pleased Ma who thought I was turning sociable, a new trend in my amorphous life.

I have to admit that there were times when the exchanging game got out of hand. I got requests for goods that nobody wanted to spare while I hated to say 'not possible'. Fortunately for me, the brothers were so busy cramming for their final exams that they did not hear of the new tricks of my trade. They did not even notice that their tennis racquet had changed colour or the little compass which my father had bequeathed to them was gone. Ma sometimes shouted at us to go down on fours and find a missing trinket or pen. Naturally, nothing would be found.

From exchanging what I had but did not want (though Ma might) for something I did not have but had to acquire without spending money, it soon became a mind game. I was sometimes juggling between three different deals and even ended up with replicas, maybe in a different colour or design, or oddities that returned after changing many hands. Nandita started learning music because she got a flute and I wore shoelaces that glowed in the dark without considering what good those can ever be.

Ma complained that the handle of the kitchen saucepan had freakishly become shorter while her green purse looked blue. Ah! Those were little switches that Nandita and I did purely for fun. Our mothers were good friends and expected us to be the same, but until the first exchange of book for football, we had not found anything in common.

'I am sure Nandita keeps a toothbrush in our house,' Ma would grumble under her breath, finding five children at the breakfast table when she was struggling with four breakfasts and lunch boxes.

'I do,' Nandita assured her, unmindful that Ma was embarrassed at being heard. She then went so far as to roar in laughter when Ma peered curiously at the saucepan. I suppose she did much the same at her house where their family saucepan had spookily grown! Before the mothers had a chance to figure out that their utensils were not indeed theirs, we intended to switch them back to their rightful kitchens, confusing matters further. The brothers avoided the two of us like we were lepers.

'Absolutely juvenile!' Amar declared calmly while we giggled.

'You may be too ashamed to be your age. We *are* juvenile, in case you haven't noticed,' Nandita told him clearly. She had read enough books to find a tongue in her mouth every time the brothers tried to put me down. To me, this was substantial reason enough to maintain a friend like her. There need be a cat to scare the mice a little.

'Is that a sleeping bag I saw you roll up this morning?' Arun asked innocently. The brothers always found a way to get even inspite of their heads being contaminated by books all the time.

'A sleeping bag?' Ma banged the alien saucepan with its scrambled eggs on the table. 'How did you get a sleeping bag?' she asked me.

Nandita nodded quickly at me. 'It is a birthday gift from her,' I told Ma.

'An old sleeping bag? You are both juvenile and cheap,' said Amar, glad to finally bite back.

Ma looked at Nandita who held out her plate for a second helping having already spooned down the first. Ma then scrutinised me. We were just plain lucky that day. The sleeping bag did belong to Nandita, bought during one of her mother's attempts to make her a child of nature. She had even taken put it to use once during a school trip she had been forcibly signed up for, the whole experience so distasteful that the sleeping bag had stayed forgotten under her cot for years.

I could see Ma silently debating whether to bring up the matter with Nandita's mother. We waited for the verdict while silently tucking in the eggs. Ma knew that if the woman had sanctioned the gift, it would be rude to say anything even if it were an old used sleeping bag which ought to be accepted gratefully since the thought did count in these matters; however, if it were not known to Nandita's mother, her mention might seem like a rude reminder of the fact that a brand new gift was not given for my birthday or worse, that we were shamelessly asking for one. The decision was easy. She decided to ignore the matter.

I revelled in the sleeping bag which was an adult size in dull green. I could easily slither all the way inside after being zipped up like a cocoon and pretend to be drowning in a green sea. It was spread atop my mattress all the time and when Ma flung it aside, I complained of sleeplessness. After three nights of me walking around the house through the night, Ma grudgingly let the sleeping bag return to my bed.

Pa was philosophical when she complained. 'Maybe she will grow too fat for it, or too long. She can't stay in it forever,' he reasoned.

'That is not the point!' Ma told him. 'She is not a child anymore and this ridiculous obsession with that filthy sleeping bag is driving me insane. Why is she so rebellious? She must have inherited it from your side of the family.'

'Just wash the silly thing,' he suggested, pragmatically steering clear of controversy.

'I did. That does not change the fact that this is a terrible habit,' she grumbled.

'It is a phase and she will outgrow it.' This turned out to be unusually insightful. Ma even wondered if he had struck a deal with me just to prove himself right.

The truth was simpler. I got a good offer to exchange the sleeping bag for a golf club that belonged to somebody's dead uncle, a long rod so shiny that I could see various distortions of my face in it. It was irresistible. I felt like a powerful gangster when I held it. I also realised that I did not miss the sleeping bag too much, my caterpillar games having become sort of weird and the pretend sea swim cramped for anything but passive drowning. I never paused to consider what I would actually do with a golf club apart from swing it around at the bushes or smack little pebbles around. Pretty soon, I was persuaded to exchange it for a little insect trapped in a jar of fruit jam.

Two days later, the insect was dead and I exchanged it for a length of some creeper that Ma had admired in Mrs Badwar's house. Her son wanted to cut the insect up to see what lay inside and I needed a cheap but impressive gift for a woman who was too proud to even ask for a piece of vine. My brothers with their extremely artistic home-made cards filled with winding verses about great mothers did not stand a chance that year for Ma's birthday. She hugged me tight and spent a whole hour wondering where to place the precious plant.

There was another bit of luck with our dead grandmother's dentures which she had relinquished over the use of vacant flexible jaws. I found them shiny and unused in her old metal trunk and a thin gloomy kid, a first-time customer, thought it an interesting possession. In return, I got a book on Indian birds with glossy pictures. Nandita grabbed the book and I came home with her entire stamp collection. Arun had one look at the stamps before quietly handing me his new denim jacket. The jacket had been a reward for his outstanding school results, a little large for me but I wore it proudly all the time with folded sleeves. Who knew false teeth could clothe people! It was baffling to the parents to understand Arun's generosity but they did not protest.

That was indeed a good year for me. I had got away with so much audacity that it never occurred to me, as it rightly should have, that I was banking on luck all the time. I had managed to sit through enough classes in school and glanced at enough pages to effortlessly clear my name in the pass list. All the while I was also getting to see, keep, use and exchange various wonderful things. The only danger was of my parents ending up with an house filled with stuff that never belonged to them, but that seemed unlikely. As we were growing independent and older, they were spending more and more time in the study, Pa desperate and Ma utterly weary. The brothers never squealed on me after the sleeping bag incident because we reached a tacit deal that I was to leave their possessions alone. Well, I mostly did. When the deal was too tempting, I did churn around a few of their belongings to be able to sneak away a thing or two and nothing was missed.

I tired of the whole game just as impulsively as it had caught my fancy. The news spread like all news is bound to. No more exchanges. The brothers were relieved especially since they had to leave for college someday and could now leave the house at my mercy. I had other concerns, other losses.

One quiet evening, Maria's father came to take her out into the winter haze. She avoided looking at the four of us and since our parents had chosen to go the club that evening rather than make goodbye speeches, she walked out quietly as if it were a walk to the grocery store. In the weeks that followed I did cry for her and made regular enquiries but was hushed up by the brothers slapping my head with cold palms. She had stayed with us over a decade, coming as a child herself to take care of those younger than her and then left one evening leaving nothing behind to remind us of her, not a shred of clothing or even a hair pin.

39

EVERYONE WAITS FOR LOVE, FOR THE ONE LOVE THAT WILL complement their fragmentary selves; for the many feeble loves that create amusement and make the passing of a dreary life bearable; for those loves that bring a rush of ardour, that dance with lust; for any love at all to make the body feel less mortal and more enduring. If not love, then affection; if not affection, maybe tolerance; for the desperate, even quiet acknowledgement will do.

We were never told to wait for love. We avoided holding hands in our family, never kissed, rarely hugged. Pa and Ma's idea of intimacy was an indulgent smile or an hour of reading out aloud from books. A lot of people don't have patience with love. Just pretty lies, they say, made up by poets and wastrels to confuse folks from the actual business of life: which is to grab a secure job, find a mate, get one kid if not more on the road to decency and hoard as many material possessions as possible.

I have never been asked if I found love and doubt if anyone ever asked the brothers. However we were frequently expected to explain: Why are all of you unmarried? Didn't your parents offer to find you companions?

No, they did not. And why should they? Raised to be single, not in any particular way but in our parents' belief that there was a better fate than marriage in store for us, we remained four pieces of a shared guilt between them. Love! Who ever thought it possible for us? It was not talked about until one of us fell in love. As usual, I was the last to know.

We were four adults perfectly content to be cooped in one house. After Ma's death, only her sister was left behind and she stuck to us simply as a filial obligation. For a while Maasi tried to tend to us, till a few years ago she declared herself to be in the process of dying and made sure we understood that she could not be bothered with us any longer. She stayed alone in a house which was less than an hour's drive from ours and despite the repeated announcements of renunciation, was extremely pleased if any of us called or visited her. We did attempt to persuade her to live with us. The sanitary ware man — it has always been hard for us to think of him as 'uncle' — had killed himself in the recent past leaving her a rich widow. There were many whispers — a mistress, mental instability, even troubled sexuality — but no suicide note with explanations. I was deeply affected by the event, amazed to discover that he had it in him to do something so dramatic. All those years we had only seen a mundane man whose emotions worked like a calculator which Ma always said was a sign of great character, but on his widow's pale face, I had seen a relief that overpowered the grief in her tears. It was a conclusive end to a relationship that Nani had made sure she could never walk away from. The only thing that had changed was that she now expected her own death and waited for it as though it would be the most logical thing to follow.

I was often deputed to visit Maasi, which I accepted without much complaints because she fed me better than the brothers did. She was also full of family albums and corresponding gossip about people I had never met but who vaguely looked a little like Ma from one angle or the other. That day I was to be dropped at her house by Arun, and though running late by an hour, was not anxious. Arun had a different watch ticking inside of him and got flustered when people fixed schedules that were dictated by the two hands on a wall clock. He was always early or late for his appointments, even if by a few minutes and with little realisation of being so. On the rare occasions when we did have to leave home as one unit of six parts, Ma always gave Arun a different reporting time than she did to the rest of us; and sure enough, he would be sitting on the front steps, genially waiting for us to catch up with him.

Arun was now smiling at himself in the rear-view mirror of the car. He swung the same smile at me as I jumped in.

The dog had followed to wag a mournful tail at me, his eyes brown and watery. I dropped a hand out of the open window and he licked my fingers thoroughly. 'Can we take him with us?' I asked Arun but was ignored. 'So broken…we are all so broken into pieces…' I muttered to the dog who, saying nothing in reply, turned around to return to his post on the two steps leading to the front door. He was capable of spending his life there, with easy access to the food inside and quick walks if someone were to go outside on any errand.

As we pulled out into the street, I turned to look at our little house which everyone said would be too little for six grown people. 'Six? What do you mean?' Pa would bark. His temper alarmingly deteriorated with age. 'Only two – me and my wife,' he would tell them. The visitors would look around at the four of us, tall hefty adults, scattered across the house and shrug their shoulders. 'Yes, of course!' – they would agree, as Ma smiled tolerantly.

We must have been expected to build our own nests. Only, nobody took the trouble. There was me, a brother holding the steering wheel tight as though it would spring out and run away, another scrubbing the kitchen stove, and a third who slept underground until the sun went down. I put both my hands in my lap and locked fingers. It probably looked like I was praying and maybe I was. The car crawled through the city traffic and not surprisingly we were the slowest. Bicycles with loads were overtaking us in congested spots. Arun, devoid of any aggression or even a semblance of it, was the worst driver of us all. He gave everyone the right of way, horse carts and buffaloes included. In Delhi, that translated to being the greatest idiot on the roads and also the last to reach anywhere at all. The lady on the car radio was fighting for airtime with the music and told us how lucky we are to have a station that gave us what our souls wanted. Not having the nerves to brave that, I turned the volume down.

'This whole Ragini business has been going on for too long…' said Arun, caving to the pressure of silence in the car. Or perhaps this was truly something on his mind. Giving him the benefit of doubt I waited for the rest, which turned out to be a question, 'Do you think Amar will marry her?'

'Who is Ragini?'

Arun shook his head in dismay. 'She comes home with Amar sometimes. You must have seen her – short hair, short girl, thin face…' he paused to think hard, 'and short hair,' he repeated, not sure if that had been mentioned.

'No,' I said, but was curious.

'Amar's boss broke his leg last year and was bed-ridden for a while. He is a seventy-year-old bachelor with only a grumpy nurse to look after him. The man was so plagued by loneliness, he said it would kill him if the festering leg did not. It really upset Amar.'

'What happened to him?'

'Oh, he had strong feelings…love, he claims…'

'For the grumpy nurse?'

'Of course not! For Ragini.'

'The old man fell in love with Ragini?'

'Amar fell in love with Ragini!'

'I mean, what happened to the old man?'

Arun took his hands off the wheel and coughed in frustration. Two loaded camel carts were blocking our car at a green signal. The animals lacked motivation to resume once they had stopped. The vehicles behind us honked as though they had landed in the street of the deaf. It was simply horrid. The cart wheels finally moved with a little help from its sweating shirtless driver. With a few seconds left for the light to turn red again, we screeched our way out of the melee.

Arun swung the car towards the outer lane into steady leisurely traffic. 'The old man still lives with the grumpy nurse, who incidentally earns more than I do! But no, it is not likely that they are in love,' said Arun. His forehead folded as he considered the possibility of a romance between the two.

'How do you know this?' I wondered.

Arun looked puzzled again. 'Well, there is no way to be entirely sure...but each time we visited the old man he did seem miserable and the nurse appeared equally unhappy with him. You will have to ask Amar to be sure.'

'Stop thinking of the nurse, will you?' I said angrily. 'I was asking – how do you know that the old man's situation inspired a romance between Amar and Ragini?'

'Oh, I don't know. It is just a theory,' he said cheerfully, to avoid having to strain himself for details out of two brief meetings with a stranger in plaster. Soon he started to whistle. I was irked to be stranded on the frontier of a conversation that had just begun to turn interesting.

There was a time when there were signs that Arun would cause trouble to Ma's vision of his perfect life. He would be reported missing from some of his tuition classes or be found in places that he never mentioned going to, odd things that caused some gladness in my heart and worry in Ma's. She then read in some magazine that every child's head is wired differently, which is the reason mathematics seems like a thing of beauty to some of us and some others can see a woman's curvy form emerging out of a big mashed up pile of clay. Arun, who did not have the ability to be organised by the hands of the clock, she deduced, had other gifts. We never quite found out about those, but among her four children, he always remained the most devoted to Ma.

We were slowly edging closer to Maasi's house. I was lost in thinking about Amar. The rest of his life was known to us, much like holding a well wrapped gift, shaking it gently and knowing from the muffled sounds, the surprise inside. In many ways his whole destiny had already been lived and by none other than his own father who was there each time he looked in the mirror. The boat Amar was taking out to check for a leak, so sanguine in his heart, had been out on the rough seas for many decades.

Everything seemed unnervingly familiar. Pa falling in love with a newspaper clipping. Needless to say, Ragini would be Ma all over again. And yet that did not happen.

I never saw any girl come home with Amar. He did not mention anything about relationships or heartbreak. Was it all a figment of Arun's imagination? Probably not. Amar looked melancholic. He kept the door of his room locked whether he was in it or not, disappeared for long walks in the night without informing us and simply forgot to smother my hair even when I went to him as dishevelled as possible.

Love must have visited my brother in vain. The human spirit is deceptive. It easily survives hurt or anger or malice only to find that the sweet wounds of love have been waiting in ambush. Pitiless. Fatal.

40

MARIA STOOD NAKED IN FRONT OF MA'S MIRROR. WE watched from Nandita's window across the road aided by the telescope I had just acquired from a profitable barter. I did most of the watching and Nandita, too excited and nervous to see for herself, let me describe aloud what I saw. Maria stood naked, staring at herself in the mirror. She put a hand to a round swollen breast and cupped it from below, caressing its honey brown tip with a thumb. She tilted her head, knowing it made her look attractive and smiled seductively at her reflection. It smiled back.

Nandita wanted to know – what is she doing now? And now?

I tried to keep up with Maria's hands. The hand that was touching her stomach, rubbing its little dome, moving down to the dark tapering patch of hair, down till her fingers disappeared. I had not yet learnt enough words to describe the look on Maria's face. Nandita pushed me aside to see for herself.

Maria stood naked before the boy from the milk booth. She loved her body and the power it gave her over trembling stripped men. Maria stood naked before the gaze of our limp gardener who scattered flower petals over her skin before crushing it with his own body. Maria stood naked before the school watchman when Nimmi rang the bell in school. But Maria was happiest when she stood naked before the mirror.

When everyone pestered Maria to disclose the name of the man who had planted the trouble in her stomach, she cried each time but never replied. The gardener disappeared. The school watchman swore to Nimmi on his bottle of liquor, never to be unfaithful again. The boy from the milk booth whined as we walked to the canopy theatre for the latest blockbuster – Is it mine? Is it mine? Is it mine?

Maria truly did not know. She must have wished it had been the mirror.

41

The Gulmohar, also known as Royal Poinciana, Flamboyant Tree, Flame Tree, Peacock Flower.

Family: Caesalpiniaceae	Genus: Delonix
Species: Regia	Category: Tropicals/Tender Perennials
Sun Exposure: Full Sun	Bloom Colour: Red

Bloom Time: Late Spring/Early Summer/Mid Summer
Foliage: Evergreen. Deciduous.

'Thank you very much,' I said, 'but of what use is all this gibberish to me?' The paper began to crumple into little wrinkles from the pressure of my fingers. Nandita grimaced in that ponderous way so unique to her. I straightened the paper and respectfully placed the paper back on her writing table.

'I thought you might like to know about the flowers that you keep filling both our notebooks with!' Nandita exclaimed and rearranged the pens and pencils on the table one more time. She liked them aligned in a particular pattern, a code that I was yet to decipher or conform to.

The gulmohar trees are in bloom. Coinciding with our summer vacations, the cover of green across the campus has erupted into flaming red.

They wave, in their merry clusters, those little bloodied stars. They wave above our heads as we cycle early mornings down empty roads. They wave their flamboyant feathery leaves into cryptic shadows below our feet as we run down the lawns with our skipping ropes. They wave their lissom bodies while dropping petals that became scarlet carpets. They wave and wave, never tiring, like old comrades.

'If you have to collect something, try stamps or coins!' Nandita exclaimed. 'Or if it has to be flowers, try to find something less common, will you? The gulmohars are everywhere. They are too boring!'

'I don't collect the flowers. Just the petals. The one petal,' I corrected her.

The aberrant petal. Each gulmohar flower has five petals, attached in a bowl shape, five creased petals separated by ten bright red stamen. Four petals like sisters, looking alike and sympathetic to a vibrant red cause but the fifth is inevitably the rebel. White on the inside, a petal shaped like a claw, white dabbed with yellow and streaked with red; tears of blood dripping down the one who dares to be individualistic. Contrariety, I insist, has never been celebrated better in nature.

The gulmohars had become an inseparable part of our lives and our friendship. During the day they captured our kites and refused to let go. In the night they nodded their heads to the angry summer skies, rising and sinking with the wind. I told Nandita that I was a collector too, same as those who picked sea-shells or gathered autographs. I was a collector of petals, of difference.

42

ON A CLOUDY AFTERNOON, AS I AMBLED IN FROM NANDITA'S house, Ma called out to me from her room. She was sitting fully dressed in her bed, as she did so often those days, undecided whether to roll out into the busy world to play her part or just succumb to the weariness inside. She had made a habit of leaning towards the window to anxiously scan the streets. Nobody was expected to visit and nothing apart from the usual happened outside our gates. Yet she continued to look out and sigh. On days when the same streets satisfied her, she would resolutely and gracefully sail out, her purse swinging to her stride. We never could predict the days when she stood erect, gritty and serene in her determination to unfold time; nor could we know when she compressed herself into a limp defeated shadow, refusing to have anything to do with us.

The memories of the cane stood between Ma and me. She thanked the cane for my upbringing and I just avoided both of them for fear that the smouldering rage in me might show, or worse, erupt. That afternoon, Ma leaned over her cot as I wobbled past her door towards my room, 'I am still alive and I am glad to see that you are too,' she said in her very sweetest voice, fake but lethal.

I wondered briefly whether to bolt, decided against it and stood politely by the door where the rest of the conversation unfurled.

'I was with Nandita,' I shrugged.

'Yes, you were,' she said a little softly. 'What are you reading these days?'

'Reading?' I wondered if that was one of those trick questions that Ma had a good stock of, 'reading...hmm... Nandita is reading *War and Peace*. She has been reading it for two months now. Someone probably did nothing else in their life but write that one book...'

'Not Nandita. You. What are you reading?' she insisted. It surprised me a little. She had never asked me that before.

'Nothing,' I told her honestly.

'I have been trying to find some books of mine. They are missing. Would you know about it?' she asked quietly. I knew then that she had stumbled upon my past as an exchange artist. Was she also aware that I had not traded in anything for over a year?

'Not one or two...but so many...' she said and I knew it could not be all my handiwork. I had just taken a couple of old books from her bookshelf, the ones that might have belonged to our infant years, stories of goblins and bean stalks. The rest were all tall words on dusty paper that I could not even pronounce. Who would want to make bedtime reading of chemistry? Even as she scrutinised my face, I tried to quickly assess if she was using exaggeration as a tool. Or was this leading to a talk about something else?

'Is there anything at all you wish to tell me Aditi? I promise that I will not shout or punish you. Is there something you have done that I should know?' she probed.

What did she want me to confess to? I had no guilt to guide me to repentance. The gentle nature of her investigations was equally novel and confounding. I waited for more clues but got none.

'I wish you would read,' she slipped down to lie on her back and pulled the sheets around her, a fledgling in a big nest. 'It will tell you all those things about life that I simply forgot to.' She closed her eyes.

I could see she was tired and wanted sleep. I took a few small steps backwards and then walked away before she could find anything else to say. Ma never called out to me again for a private chat and I forgot about her lost books.

All of us in the house were in the know of the ailments that Ma suffered from. She would describe her suffering in great detail to the colleagues, students and neighbours who made courtesy visits. We also knew that she was suffering from something else that as yet did not have a name. The name came too late – death by pining for a love long lost.

an unsung song

43

THE ART DEALER HAS NOT HEARD FROM VISHNU IN MANY months and the paintings have stopped arriving at his doorstep. The patrons are restless. Where is Vishnu? What is he painting these days? Why is he hiding and wasting his gift?

Vishnu finds himself ageing and unable to continue the life of a vagabond. For years he has been a travelling artist, moving as fast as he can to avoid his reputation from catching up with him. He lives with the common people, eats their frugal food and in gratitude makes little family portraits that sit proudly on the grimy walls of their little huts. Vishnu has begun to see meaning in his work now but soon he will turn eighty and his body does not obey his will as it used to.

The dealer decides to investigate and intrude upon the man in exile. After much perseverance, he finally locates Vishnu living in a little cottage by the sea with a blind cat for company. He has not moved for two years, unable to muster the energy to pick up the easel, his bag of paints, the few clothes and books, and consign his body into the swells of humanity that spill around him and in his mind.

'Where are you storing your recent work? I can't wait to see it,' pesters the dealer in his letters.

Vishnu requests patience, 'I am working on something special. This is probably the most important series of my long artistic pursuit. Have faith.'

'Fine! But surely you can let me have a look,' and then, with pleading, ' We have been friends for so long. Don't you trust me?'

Vishnu is firm. 'I am not ready to expose them to anyone's eye but mine. It is too early.'

The dealer, a wizened man who has prospered beyond his own imagination because of the talent of an eccentric recluse, refuses to believe that waiting is the right approach. He continues to inundate Vishnu with a stream of constant letters and telegrams begging to have a preview of this new collection. Ignored for months, the man finally travels across continents to visit the artist who is lying feverish in bed under the blind cat's anxious vigil. The doctor, driven down to the cottage by the dealer, writes out some medicines for immediate relief, then proposes a medical investigation at the city hospital and perhaps a change in climate.

Vishnu gives the suggestion some thought. He has grown to like the sound of the waves and the long months of incessant rains. He likes to walk barefoot on the beach in the evenings, stand at the fringe of the waves for hours, and then come home to flick each sticky grain of sand off his feet, one by one. Why would anyone renounce a life of such beauty?

The dealer and the doctor join hands to impress good sense on the old man. They tell him of the risks involved in ignoring sound advice. After days of refusing, Vishnu wakes up one day with the vision of a remote valley in the heart of white mountains.

'I will move and also get the tests done, but,' he cautions the relieved dealer, 'some arrangements will have to be made and I want a house to be built specially for me.'

A house for an artist! The news passes around — for the dealer does little else but sit with a tiny blinking phone pressed against his cheek — and architects compete with each other in offering their expertise, with or without any promise of payment. Vishnu picks the one with the least reputation and instructs that his sea-side cottage be recreated down to the smallest detail in the valley.

'The blind cat was living in this house when I moved in and should not be inconvenienced by the relocation,' he explains.

The architect gets up to go but is asked to sit down again. There would be one significant addition. Adjacent to the house, a circular structure has to be constructed: it will have only one door and no windows; a private art gallery of cream coloured walls, with the best wall lights and spatial dimension possible.

The harried dealer just finishes finalising the paperwork with the architect when Vishnu begins asking for a lawyer. 'A will has to be drawn,' he says simply.

There is much wealth to leave behind but it is all contained in a few details. All he owns, he is willing away to an ashram in some remote place that neither dealer nor lawyer has heard of — all except the private painting gallery beside his house. That, he decides, will be thrown open for public viewing after his death and be managed by a Trust. Till then nobody would be allowed to see any of its exhibits.

'As for you my old friend,' Vishnu tells the dealer who is fatigued from battling with the artist's demands and is slumped low on the porch trying to call his airlines to confirm the ticket back home, 'after my death, you will take good care of my cat, won't you?'

44

I GLANCE AGAIN AT MY ESCORT. A YOUNG BOY, ALMOST MAN, fitted in a white driver's uniform, a size too large for him. He delicately floats inside it, his body nimble and face radiantly pink as comes from being born in the mountain air. He nods at me shyly and wipes the seats with a rag dirtier than the upholstery. I have waited through seasons for this day. A lot of convincing had to be done. Nobody thinks any good can come out of my meeting an artist who is known to be quirky. Luckily none could say for sure that it would be harmful either.

'Nonsense!' said the Great Sister. 'Another of her self-indulgent ploys. This is the trouble with brats who are born with every comfort and don't have to work for their meals.'

It may help her – pondered the authorities – or it may not.

'Why will some famous artist who has spent all his life avoiding people want to meet her?' the brothers reasoned. 'If he does, let him do so at his own risk. We have nothing more to say.'

Finally, the matter was settled when my letter to the artist received a reply after weeks of waiting.

The letter said, 'Come.'

The car is ready. I hold my hat, gather my skirt and slide in next to the boy. My blood warms steadily from the excitement. Soon even the thin shawl on my shoulders is like a blanket and I shrug to let it slip off. As we rattle over the gravelled pathway of the estate, a nippy breeze enters the moving vehicle with decisive calm. I am back in the open free world. Trees, roads, mountains and streams steadily unfurl and run past my window. I squint at the explosion of sights and little tears gather at the corner of the eyes from both strain and elation.

'Am I going too fast?' the boy asks with concern.

I shake my head, 'No, no. Can you go faster?'

'No. This is as fast as I can go,' he apologises.

'Then this is just fine,' I smile.

The views race at a happy pace. The hills look sleepy under the shy sun. Villagers standing by the roadside wave vigorously, their lips pleading with us to take them along. I wave back in greeting. They look disappointed but the boy has been strictly told not to stop till we reach the artist's house. His other instructions are equally simple: wait patiently when you get there, keep a casual but steady eye on the girl and return well before dusk.

45

THERE WHERE THE CEDARS GROW VERY TALL, AND THE sunlight forgets to slide deep enough to touch the sand, I hear his heart beat. There the moss spreads like a deep sorrow, thick over the pebbly banks. There falling leaves touch his shoulders and then his feet. There the stream says little, yet sighs with the constantly writhing mist. There he lives his last days, waiting for the stranger he is meant to love.

Our car swings into a valley that is tightly packed with cedars, every inch of space splashed in green. We are raising dust in the quiet settlement. Lean muscular women carry bundles of branches on their heads; a few children mind goats that are too lazy to graze; old men read different pages of the same newspaper through thick dusty glasses. Beyond the few cluttered huts, I sight the slanting tiles of his roof, replicating a distant sea-side cottage and courageously locking its gaze with the stately snow-topped peaks.

46

HE IS WATCHING THE WOODS. HIS EYES FLICKER LIGHTLY only when a pine needle succumbs to the seductive wind to float away. The same wind invades my skirt and does not stop till it strikes bone. It also reaches his fingers which shiver while the rest of him stays still. Those fascinating fingers! They hang loosely, pointing downwards, slightly bent at each joint, slender enough to break at the will of the wind but with so much assurance that I expect the ground to jump up any moment to grasp them. Paintbrushes made of flesh, ten of them, brown and taut like a child's. A little of the palms flash, white pieces of ice that have never seen blood. Neither blood nor lines. Where does this man store his destiny? His forehead is broad and speaks of no worry. His feet are bare but supple. His hair hangs long, a mane as white as his palms. He is tall but not lanky. He is thin but not bony. He is not happy but not sad either. He accepts my entry in his house but does not acknowledge it with speech. He is ageless and I feel my heart opening up to the skies. There is warmth is my toes and behind my ears. My lungs forget to expand or collapse. The stream is now flowing through me, the cedars are growing in my spine and the butterflies are falling asleep in my head. A tear singes my face. I long to feel, caress and experience this man with my entire self.

He gets up, turns away from my longing and walks into the house. I draw my feet into the old comforting huddle to brace my overflowing emotions.

He returns with a round glass tray that he gently puts down between us. The brief craving for his skin now breaks and whimpers to an early death inside me. Our smiles meet. It is only now I become aware of what I have forgotten to wait for all these years and only after it has humbled me with a swift exit.

I don't drink tea but know that I now should. He lifts the lid of the pot to see if the leaves have brewed. A long strand of steam licks his nose. I smell it too, a nameless fragrance the earth reluctantly releases into a sombre night.

'A cup of tea,' he says each word with care, straining neither face nor voice, 'is an experience. These leaves that swim in hot water so briefly to release their flavours before we throw them away, they have to be treated with respect. I don't like to belittle that by adding milk or sugar but I can get you some if you wish.'

'No, thank you. I will have my tea the same as you.' I hastily reach out for the first cup that the lean spout fills but hesitate to drink. Is there something equally profound about waiting for the dark liquid to cool itself? Why is he sitting so still, staring deep into his cup?

'Vishnu,' I whisper.

He looks at me with a captivating smile. 'Why did you want to see me?'

'I have many questions for you.'

He bends his head a little and lifts it up again with another smile, this time in his eyes. He is waiting to be asked.

'I am sorry but I cannot remember any now,' I confess softly. He nods in understanding and sips his tea slowly. I taste mine. It is warm, bitter, aromatic, intoxicating. Entirely magical. I had never imagined a little tea could make me want to weep like a child. But it does! A long tea leaf has escaped from the pot and now flounders at the bottom of my cup. I watch it rest with a little swirl. My head bends complaisantly for another sip, careful not to disturb the leaf. The artist seems to approve because he talks again.

'It takes a frightfully lonely person to achieve an original and genuine vision.'

'In art?'

'Art. Life. It is the same. You have to embrace the loneliness, there is no other way.'

'How will I survive it?'

'I look at the sky,' he tells me, 'at space.'

'And you paint…' I say hesitantly.

He puts his cup down and starts walking. I hurry behind him, ruing my impulsive words. You are an ass — I tell myself — with no esteem for the man's wisdom. He clearly does not want to talk about his work. He speaks as though the words are pearls stringing themselves into a necklace in his mouth, the meaning so easy to miss in the very beauty of hearing them spoken.

'Why does anything have to be achieved? All achievement is at the cost of something else, someone else. For every victor, there are many pained and vanquished. The glory is always stolen. It is the non-achiever, the non-doer who holds the keys to happiness.'

We step around to face the house from its side and I realise there is no neighbour. The sloping roof of the house stands alone, the wilderness clamouring at it. A small patch of clearing is all that separates it before mounds of earth rising high with their load of bark and leaves. I can see nothing of the view that had run alongside the car on our journey here, the profusion of hills falling all over each other for miles. It would be easy to believe, standing where I am, that there is no land beyond this little pocket of greenery that surrounds the house, so perfect is its isolation. I continue to walk beside Vishnu as a whistling thrush hops across our heads, shrilly longing for a mate. He wordlessly points it out to me and I nod in admiration.

Two labourers by the fence greet us. They are sitting in the grass, hewing planks and bend low to the ground as we pass.

'Bhola and Sadhu, our local carpenters...' Vishnu introduces. 'They make frames to mount the canvas cloth. I take a lot of time to decide the size of a painting. Often, I am not sure till I actually dip my brush in paint.'

'Can I...?' I wonder and hesitate to say more.

'See the paintings?' He stops walking and knits his eyebrows critically before pointing to the circular building about which so much has been written about in the papers. 'It is all in there. You can see it when you want to. But do you really want to?'

'No.' I bow my head in shame.

We have now completed a circle and stop in front of the house where the driver is sleeping across the front seat of the car, his feet sticking out from an open door. We walk past him silently. Vishnu is sailing and does not look to guide his bare feet. I gather my long skirt in two fistfuls to keep pace.

'Surely it must mean something that so many people understand and wait for your work,' I say as we return to the tables in the backyard. The cups of tea have mysteriously disappeared. Is there someone else in the house watching us?

He shakes his head sadly. 'Every art movement of significance questions the norms and rules of its times. A true artist in search of truth often explores that which is exactly opposite to what his contemporaries believed in — to question the rules, rebel and then emerge with a fresh voice. It might bring him fame and attention. It might not. Every trend negates the previous one. But these are the times of no rules and chaos survives in the name of individuality. The artist has nothing to challenge but his own fate of being born in an age of confusion.'

'And if confusion is challenged, what would be the negation of confusion?' I wonder. 'Order?'

'No…more confusion…maybe destruction…'

I turn round another bend of the house but he is walking straight through the grassy patch into the nearest cover of trees. My body sways once with uncertainty before trailing him, an enigmatic urgency in every step and a need to be as close to him as I can. Soon we are walking through the pathless spaces between the gigantic trees. He leads in silence, precisely one step ahead of me. As our feet crunch over the thick undergrowth, it is impossible to continue talking as before or even to pull apart far enough to look at his face. As the trees crowd together and lean over to nuzzle each other, my body is invariably attached to one side of his. I don't know when my arm slips through his but it does. We are walking as one. And soon the woods are breaking into a little clearing.

Vishnu stops at a stone bench. It is an object of elegance, every inch stroked and shaped by a man's chisel, by the very hands that I hold in mine. We sit in silence. The forest waits on us watchfully. I look up at the sky but it is gone. On the fringes of the calm treetops is a hole filled with light, a very diffused blue lustre, turning green as it descends, melting into sparks of brown as it disappears under our feet. It is the light of calm.

For the first time, I know that I'm breathing deeply.

The brush of life travels over mountains, oceans, deserts, plains, with a flourish that invites the air to rush in with life. I breathe that life in.

For the first time I see the unseen. The unconditional. I see love.

Without being told, I am told what is One. What came out of my mother for the fourth disappointing time and what fell out of Maria is One.

For the first time, I taste the milk of earth in my throat. It is also the tears mortality sheds for its own helplessness.

The dragonfly alights at my feet. Its ruby eyes are missing. Into the empty bottomless sockets now fills my father's blood. Drop by drop.

To live is to wait. To wait is to open the mind. To open the mind is to be an artist. To be an artist is to breathe. And I know why I breathe.

Vishnu is walking away from the stone bench. I get up to follow but linger as far behind as possible without losing sight of his gliding white shirt. I imagine some merciful bush will grab my feet, sink inextricable thorns in my flesh and never let go. I would want nothing more than to be rooted here forever.

The house is soon visible and the car where the young man is earnestly scrubbing the windshield clean for the journey. Vishnu is waiting patiently for me to catch up. He looks pale and melancholic. The lines and wrinkles in his body are bending low to hide the fatigue of a long and demanding life. I perceive it, and for that he smiles at me. His face transforms into a circle of light, no different than the halo above the clearing we have left behind.

'Why did you agree to see me?' I want to know, but he shrugs the question away. I wonder if he expects more formality and propriety. 'You must be very busy,' I say humbly.

'The reputation keeps people away. I need the day for painting and the night for resting. Where is the time for anything else?' His voice is kind, trying to tell me not to try too hard to make separation endurable. The hurt will always be real and belong to both of us while the pretence is doomed to be all mine.

'You made time for me,' I say shyly and with gratitude.

He bends down and touches his lips lightly to mine, soft and delicate, a drizzle of nectar. I want to throw my arms around the kindly neck, soak in his strength and kiss him back. I find myself unable to move. Vishnu is gently bundling me into the car which leaves the valley as quickly as the failing light and curving roads allow. It takes only one lithe bend of the road to lose forever the view of the cottage.

47

PAINTED IN WHITE, WORDS BORROWED FROM TAGORE'S *Gitanjali*, a brown wooden board hangs at the entrance of a private art gallery in a remote valley of the Himalayas: *The song that I came to sing remains unsung to this day. I have spent my days in stringing and in unstringing my instrument.*

There where the cedars race with the dusk to create prisons of wood, my desires get caught. There the secrets of a lifetime can be contained, but soon they will evaporate. There unfasten the knots of yesterdays, to be recognised, remembered and then forgotten for ever. There leaves will continue to fall on his shoulders, his feet. There a part of me has decided to stay behind.

birds fly and fish swim

48

TIME IS NOW MY CONSTANT COMPANION AND WE HAVE BOTH moved into the wide room where the twins once stayed. The walls are freshly painted pink and the windows are covered by a thin wire mesh. The hills swing themselves between laboriously making snow and then melting it. I don't look for respite from Time anymore. Every day lives itself. The hours are no different than little rain drops now and I shall stir for nothing less than a deluge.

49

'I WAS THERE LAST NIGHT.'

'Where?'

'In their room. I watched them but they did not notice me. They were busy…'

'The twins? And what happened then?'

Late in the night when all footsteps had died in the Big House, I stood at their door. It had swung wide enough for me to watch without being discovered. The tall open windows were flooding the walls and floor with moonlight. I stood as dead as the door fixtures. After the darkness of my own room and the corridors, the silvery highlights were harsh and disturbing. I saw one twin and then the other, both on their knees, scrapping off pieces from the wall, intently eliminating their drawings, some made barely a few inches above the floor when they were just toddlers.

190   birdswim fishfly

Yes, I was there, watching for a long serpentine hour, breathing quietly, braving the cold, immobile when instinct urged me to stamp on my feet or blow warm air into frozen fingers. I did not have the courage to risk interrupting those steady repetitive sounds – scratch, erase, peel, smudge, wipe, smear, daub, fade, scrape – resolute but violent little hands at work.

My muscles turned stiff from the fright of watching those countless drawings I so admired being methodically destroyed. The twins did not notice me or the silent pleadings of my horrified eyes that they spare at least the little patch of flowers by the curtains where I had been installed as a midget, where for the only time in my life I had golden hair. I looked away in pain when they scrubbed me to a blur.

They laboured furiously, moving away from each other along the wall. The paintings towards the ceiling being more recent and rich with detailing demanded more chipping unlike the fruits, birds and stick figures at the bottom of the walls. Pieces of paint and plaster kept falling softly around their feet. The boys never looked up and never took a break. They worked with concentrated thoroughness.

I turned around and quietly hobbled back to bed, not because the cramps in my feet were excruciating, but only because my heart was breaking in too many places, into too many pieces.

50

I HAD JUST COLLAPSED INTO MY PILLOW AND SNUGGLED close to the darkness of the night. Among the few things I had learnt to enjoy as the years swept over our parental roof, were dreams: grand fantasies jostling with comforting daily details to entertain me with their spectral brilliance. My mind had just sunk into a burgundy cloud when all the lights were turned on in the room.

'Wh…what…what happened?' I mumbled, unable to open my eyes to the combined brightness of five bulbs. The incubating dreams scampered for cover leaving behind distress.

'Aditi, did your mother tell you anything about her jewellery?' I heard Maasi's voice.

'Let her sleep,' Anand was saying. 'This is ridiculous! Maasi, why have you rounded us up like sheep in the middle of the night? We can have this meeting in the morning, can't we? I am going back to bed…'

'No, not in the morning. Now!' she insisted. 'Wake up, Aditi! Arun, please hand me that glass of water.'

I struggled with the bed clothes and managed to open one eye. The brothers were standing near the door, leaning sleepily against the walls. Only our militant aunt looked alert and capable of springing out of the window for a quick morning flight. Through the thin curtains was the dense and compressed darkness of a starless night. Two street-lamps created convoluted shadows of our house on the trees and the trees duplicated their blotched shapes through our open windows on the inner walls of the house.

Maasi had agreed, after much persuasion, to spend a weekend with us, most of which she spent talking to us as Ma would, pointing to all that never got done as efficiently as they should be and suggesting some more slavery to the daily routine. Meeta Maasi, once so glad to be different from her sister, even if to be a bumbling homely cliché, had finally slipped into the iron mould, but being a poor imitation of the original, I still found her very loveable.

Amar took a step forward and put an arm around Maasi to suggest that she leave. 'You must have dreamt of something,' he said kindly. 'Why this sudden concern for non-existent jewels?'

'Non-existent!' she gasped. 'I never asked before because I thought you children were responsible enough to take care of everything after your mother's death. Somehow I could not sleep tonight…you know, with so many burglaries in the neighbourhood. And then I realised that I should check with you to see if they have been put away safely.'

'Ma never wore anything of value,' Arun said. The other two brothers quickly endorsed that.

'Ha!' she snorted. 'Just because she did not wear anything does not mean that she did not own them! Your grandmother, my mother, gave her a lot of antique gold that belonged to our grandmother. And then, she had those diamonds and emeralds, so very beautiful, and surely priceless.'

I was wide awake now and so were the others. Here we were, living frugal lives thanks to a mother who wrote down every spent rupee in a little notebook and made sure we felt adequately guilty for every acquisition, only to be told a few years later that all the while she was an undercover empress with flashy jewels. The picture of an ascetic Ma somehow did not match with this revelation. It seemed highly improbable.

Amar interjected, 'Where would she get the diamonds and emeralds and everything else you imagine from? I can't believe it! Pa never made enough money and Ma never showed interest in anything but her books. After she died we found nothing but some trinkets of little value. Even the earrings she wore every single day of her life were fake. I don't understand any of this. If she did have these jewels, like you say, don't you suppose she might have kept them in some safe place?'

'No, she would not agree to that. I used to always nag her about hiring a bank locker but she wanted to have them close to her, to look at when she wished. For all her intellectual high-mindedness, your mother was a big sentimentalist…a fool!'

I had never heard anyone say that about Ma; our sensible, cerebral, rational flame of feminine energy. There is just so much that children never find out about their parents. We waited to hear more but the woman was now struggling with her conscience. We could see the question on her face – do I tell more or do I keep shut?

'Oh! Tell us!' Anand tried to tip the scales. 'You will be doing Ma a favour if those things really meant so much to her.'

'I don't know. She never wanted to talk about it and certainly not to her children. So maybe I should not say any more than I have…' She looked worried and turned to the wall to consider the matter without the four pair of eyes drilling into her face.

'The precious jewellery...' I mentioned to speed up a resolution to the moral dilemma and it worked. Maasi was burdened with some remnants of the sanitary ware-man's good sense in her. She turned to us with confidence. Something of value was at stake and that unfailingly became more important than keeping promises to the dead.

'A little before she met your father, your Ma had met someone else. How can I say this...' she hesitated.

'A lover?' I offered.

'An admirer,' she snapped resolutely. 'Vikram loved Sujatha to distraction. To begin with they were strangers. In fact, I was present during their first meeting – at a concert hall. He kept staring at her from the moment we walked in though she did not spare a glance. Of course I did not understand her disinterest. Our friends were always telling us about him, the most sought-after young man those days, so good-looking and charming, and his father, who owned the biggest jewellery store in the city, was as rich as a king!

'Wherever Sujatha went, there Vikram was, just worshipping her with his eyes and always from a respectable distance. To begin with, it irked her. Once she even confronted him, or so she claimed, and then something happened between them. I'm not sure... Your Ma became so secretive. I knew she met him often but something was not quite right. She was disturbed by many things about him, especially the family wealth that he was dependent on. Poor Vikram was one of those born not to earn a living but to spend an inheritance. I also know that he gave her many gifts. She would refuse and get angry with him but he pleaded with her to keep them.

'They were mostly precious stones set in such unique designs that the mind trembles to even imagine. I never saw Sujatha wear any of them. Instead, she would give it to me for safekeeping. I was younger but certainly the more responsible one. Every single gift was exquisite and surely worth a fortune.'

She paused to revive her own girlhood memories of wonderment, the sensation of looking deep into the gleaming eye of a sapphire or the thrill of slipping a diamond pendant into her cleavage in the privacy of the bathroom where she secretly shared objects of love that belonged to her sister. We spotted a warm flush on her elderly face and waited politely, pretending we had not.

'Your Pa married your Ma. We never heard of Vikram again,' she winded up dryly.

'This is preposterous!' said Amar. 'And does not sound like Ma!'

'Are you suggesting that I am a liar?' she glared at him.

'Why didn't Ma tell us where she kept the jewellery? She had thought of everything before her death, every single detail from grocery lists to legal papers. If she kept them safely, why didn't she tell us?' Arun wondered aloud.

Everyone sat in silence for a while. I could see Maasi struggle with her conscience.

'Oh! Tell us!' I urged her again.

'I am not sure, but I just remembered a conversation I had with your mother. She was telling me about Aditi's habit of sneaking things out of the house. She worried about you, Aditi. I think she once told me something about how she didn't want a mischief to be labelled as theft. She said reputations matter more than jewellery...'

I had heard enough and slipped back under the sheets. The conversation became unimportant to me. I had heard Ma's complaints so many times over the years and was not ashamed of those ingenious exchanges that had given me a short period of acceptance in the world. From under the blanket I waited to hear the end of that recollection but it never came. Maasi's voice had trailed off. The boys were walking out of the room, taking her with them. I heard the lights being turned off. The dog, now woken by the commotion, sauntered into the room and climbed on my bed. I cuddled close to him for warmth. The night again collapsed into a black stillness.

51

HE LOVED HER IN THE LIGHT OF THE SAPPHIRE SPARKLING on her bare skin when she turned on her side beside him. She wore nothing but that drop of glowing blue, her breasts rising like waves under their hypnotic lure. He put a hand on her stomach and watched his fingers make little dips in her flesh as she sighed and smiled in her sleep.

He loved her till his body ached without respite, till his mind turned numb to everything but the swing of her hips as she ran down the library steps towards him, till his heart had to be nudged into every beat. He loved her till it was impossible to be anything but her shadow. He followed her wherever she went.

He loved her but never found out if she loved him just as much. She smiled at him, her eyes like pools of light reflecting the warm flush of her cheeks. He knew she smiled that way at none else but him. Did she love him like he did? That night in bed, she wore the emeralds at her throat and set him on green fire.

He loved her and craved for her every waking moment, through every drop of sleep. The love forbade him from saying anything when she told him that ideals meant more than emotions and she had met a man who could give her that life she deserved. She held out a velvet pouch to him and he knew his love was in it. Keep it – he begged her. They are much too precious – she said sadly, for she wished they had been just glass and fit to be thrown away. Not more precious than you – he wept. How could his love walk away with nothing of him? Keep it – he begged.

He never stopped loving her. He watched her often, always making sure that she never knew of it. He kept his vigil on her home, her growing family, her greying hair and the fatigue of a loveless isolation in her steps. He knew he had to somehow let her know that his love was waiting for her return.

52

SOMETIMES, I WOULD OPEN AN OLD BOOK AND A DRIED gulmohar petal would waft down to the floor. I never bothered to pick it up and restore it into its vault of words. Why should I? The petals of dissent had ceased to have any meaning or beauty for me. I did not collect them anymore but not because the flowers had stopped blooming around me. I simply chose not to notice the lush blossoms and for that there was a wooden spatula to blame. It had wrecked havoc in our young lives, more than Nandita or I'd ever thought likely.

Laila had complained herself hoarse. If they had been my children, I would make sure they knew right from wrong – she rumbled.

Ma brought the cane down on me with frustrated fury – when will this girl learn? When will she let me live in peace? – and only then did I realise that she too wanted to be free of the cane but did not dare depend on chance to straighten me to her satisfaction. We were both equally trapped.

Determined to doing the right thing, Ma dragged me to Nandita's house with Laila in sulky tow. Her parents listened to the story, horrified. Ma saw their accusing silent eyes fall on me: their daughter had been a paragon of goodness till I had come along.

'You are sorry for what you did, aren't you?' Ma asked Nandita.

'No,' said Nandita plainly, and refused to reconsider the matter.

We returned home in silence and I was told to apologise for both Nandita and myself which I quickly did. A few weeks later, Nandita was packed off to a very reputed but distant residential school. Her parents did not want to take a chance on me either. Before Nandita left, we spent our last few days together away from all adults, under the gulmohar trees, cursing the insensitivity in others and the helplessness of our young years. She promised to be back in six months for her vacations.

I waited impatiently for her return and when she did, it was not as I had anticipated. Nandita had grown taller, paler, and held herself with a natural aloofness from all objects and people around her, including me. All my ebullience was met with a quiet patience and a detachment that first puzzled and then pained me. The heroism I had sought in her was probably something she missed in me. Or perhaps an unnamed force had broken into my only friend's spirit. She avoided me and in a few days I too learnt to look the other way when she walked past our house holding her mother's hand. Summer was at its prime and the gulmohars were in vigorous bloom but neither of us looked at them anymore.

53

THE SUN CLOSED ITS EYES. THE WINDOW SWUNG BACK TO trap the little twilight it could. The curtains fell into mute folds. There is no light in his heart; there should be no light in his world.

He pulled open a drawer. The knife had been put there months ago, on a similarly bleak day. He raised his hand over his table and rested it lovingly upon the bed of papers. Before him was his life's work, now just pieces of paper. Inside him, fading hope. There was desire but the ability to define it was missing. He looked at the veins, swollen but taut, running like criss-crossed railway tracks on the fair surface of his broad open wrists.

His palms folded into fists. The blue stood out. He did not look at the blade of the knife as it sank into the nervous lines. He did not mind the red that ran into delirious patterns on books he studied with so much care. He did not hear his wife scream her horror at him. He did not hear the white doctor comforting, reprimanding, prescribing medicines.

Instead, Pa saw withered murky brown dahlias bloom in his mind. Through the window of his study, he saw the strong green stem of flowers that have not grown in years. Yellow petals bouncing yellow sunlight. The whole universe turned into gold before his eyes.

Depression, Ma heard the doctor tell her about the man lying pale in her bed.

'It makes no sense at all,' she said. 'I am the one with the broken heart.'

54

SHE TOOK ME ALONG, ONE OF THOSE SUMMER AFTERNOONS when I wished to go back to the canopy theatre and later lie about having been at the park. Strangely, there was no sign of the boy from the milk booth and we were walking in the opposite direction.

'Maria, where are we going?'

'Nowhere, my darling.'

We walked through the streets till my feet ached and I sat on a dirty pavement rock to complain. She waved frantically to a cycle-rickshaw. Maria had to argue and bargain with the tall ugly man who peddled over to us: 'Be reasonable! It's not that far and you can't count this frail child as a whole person.' He scowled at me and smiled lopsided at Maria. 'Pay what you want to,' he told her. Soon we were settled behind him, meandering around the lanes of the city. I was pleased.

'Maria, where are we going?'

'To my old neighbourhood. Don't worry dear. I have a little business to take care of. We will be home soon.'

The cycle-rickshaw struggled to manoeuvre his patched worn-out tyres through the teeming traffic. The old crumbly buildings came into view, mended with some new cement appendages, growing closer and closer to each other, till they turned into two towering and intimidating walls on both sides of us. Walls, from which people leaned out to spit on the roads and to breathe in the polluted air. The rickshaw jumped over a speed-breaker. Maria groaned and clutched her stomach, now a small circle of flesh sitting coyly in her lap. The stomach seemed to wonder just as I did.

'Maria, where are we going?'

'Here we are! Hush, my angel! We will be back home soon. Sit here and wait for me. I will not be gone for long. Can you see that room over there? I have to meet a good lady there. She will help me get better.'

The rickshaw man, however, refused to wait for our return. He took his money and leered at Maria's legs. I stepped in between the two of them and clung to her dress. He left and soon after, she disappeared down the grey corridor. I sat on a muddy rock and watched the bustle of the streets. Everyone was moving. They agreed and argued, purchased and sold, while pushing ahead of each other. They even threw a banana peel at my feet and spewed obscenities in my hearing but nobody would stop long enough to tell me why Maria had not come out as fast as she had promised. Where had she brought me? When would we be going home?

I couldn't bear to wait any longer. Surely my sweet Maria would understand and forgive my impatience. I ran up the steps, down the corridor, across doors painted bright maroon. I stumbled to that very wall where I knew a very good lady was helping my very sad friend. The door was tightly shut. I knocked. Inhuman sounds echoed back. I knocked again, louder. Through the door came cries and screams, muffled but vivid. My little heart, ready to burst open, pushed the door more desperately, so desperately that I heard a latch fall loose on the other side. I pressed myself against it and the door gave way.

Red trickled from beneath Maria's sleeping form. Blood! Her legs were folded up and drawn apart. I could not see her face, hidden by the dress bunched up around her chest. But how well I knew that dress! Maria had worn it once in the rain and protected it with an orange umbrella. Two women were bent over her like stakes.

Maria!

She cried out my name.

Her voice was dipped in the blood that sparkled on the floor. It clawed through the walls of that room. It scalded the afternoon. It burnt everything inside of me to cinders.

MA HAD ASKED, 'IS THERE ANYTHING AT ALL YOU WISH TO tell me Aditi? I promise not to shout or punish you. Is there something you have done that I should know? I expect to be told the truth.'

She had waited for a confession, for me to say that I took her precious memories of glitter thinking them to be worthless and exchanged them for a smelly glove or the inconsequential likes. I stayed silent not from guilt but ignorance. Her subtlety was squandered on me. Ma must have then decided to think me a thief rather than speak plainly.

I cannot complain. I had chosen discretion too. I had chosen not to tell.

I was in the overcoat, at the crossroads in front of our house, being hugged by a stranger, seeing nothing but darkness and hearing Maria scream in the distance. Instead of fear, there was confidence of being rescued. An abstruse instinct assured me the man meant no harm.

Inside the stranger's coat, I heard him speak, mellow and plaintive. He whispered into my hair, so softly, the words slid down my body to melt and nearly evaporate.

Tell your mother that I still love her. Tell her. I will wait for as long as she wants me to. Tell her to come to me. Will you tell her?

I nodded. He put me down gently on the road, kissed me fervently as if my lips were somebody else's and walked away, calmly wiping his tears.

Tell her...tell her...tell her...

LAILA'S MATTRESS, SO OLD THAT IT BARELY HELD TOGETHER and so stained that it was hardly any colour. Laila is dead. Her daughter-in-law wants the mattress thrown out of the house and set aflame. She had not hated the old woman as much as the gangrene on her leg. One mouth less to feed, she thinks, and one smelly mattress out of the house; her days were going to be endurable again.

Laila's lumpy mattress is lying by the roadside where her grandchildren play. The eldest, old enough to remember and miss his grandmother, has been told to drag it to the dump beyond the huts and burn it. His younger brothers and sisters want to go along for the adventure and a joy ride. The two elder boys let the little ones settle down on the mattress as they drag it along, hoping their mother won't spy them dallying from her narrow kitchen window.

Laila's mattress has uncomplainingly soaked many tears: rivers of tears that she shed when her burly husband shrunk in the face of painful prostate cancer, when a son spent months in jail for petty crimes, when two other sons disappeared to become illegal immigrants on remote lands and when a daughter died during childbirth on that very mattress. Tears were also shed when she tried hard to forget all about the house where she fed three boys and their annoying sister. Sometimes she had even cried for herself, for her festering leg, clutching her pillow and cursing her fate. Laila craved more than anything to rip her mattress apart but was daunted by the terror of her own life, her hidden agonies. I will do it later – she told herself – when I really need to.

Laila's mattress is being dragged across stones and garbage. Gurgling with delight, one of its passengers, a little girl, digs her fingers into the loosening fabric for a better grip. The ride is becoming bumpier. The mattress splits into two and the children topple along with their grandmother's secret into the sand. Scattered around them are glittering pieces of coloured stones in yellow metal and a little dragonfly with ruby eyes.

57

AMAR CALLS TO SAY THAT THE BASEMENT IS NOW EMPTY. Anand has left. Over the phone, his voice takes turns to scatter and stretch, indicating some confusion over the loss. Did Amar truly believe that all of us would grow old together in that house? How had Anand managed to find the courage to pack his bags and start a life on his own?

Amar is groping for a perspective – Perhaps we should sell the house...there are maintenance problems...the plumbing...the termites...the noisy neighbours...

What he really wants to escape, are the ever-present shadows of dead parents and the years they spent tinkering with our minds. He does not want to admit it.

'What do you think?' he wants to know.

Me? What do I think?

'You have a share in this house too you know,' he reminds me. 'Anand has said that he does not care about the house or any share in the sale proceeds.'

What happened to Anand? What happened in that basement?

'He has made a lot of money now and I think it bothers him enough to want to be alone and apart from us. It bothers me too. I have long suspected that he spends most of his time down in the basement hacking…'

That sounds violent. Not like Anand.

'It amounts to some sort of burglary. You know, on the internet…'

Burglar? One of the brothers is a burglar?

Amar is waiting for reassurance. He wants me to tell him what Ma would have directed he do: talk sense into Anand, keep the house and remember that there is nothing more important than discipline.

I take a deep breath and decide to walk the other way, 'Yes, sell the house.'

He promises to visit me soon and the phone line goes dead. It has been months now since they have asked me when I plan to return. It is understood that I will get back when I have exhausted all my reasons not to.

I am delighted. The picture on Ma's wall is changing. Soon, we shall all be free.

58

The obituaries are everywhere. He is hailed as a genius of our times, a visionary, a man of abundant gifts. Not much detail, because nothing is known of his humble beginnings, his spiritual confinement in the ashram, his nameless years and his many wanderings.

A fire has been doused. A treasure has been emptied. A man, a talent, an artist is dead — say the tributes, mostly by people who hardly knew him. The loss, they say, is irreplaceable.

Vishnu's trusted art dealer has come by the first flight possible, looking devastated, to make sure there is no violation of a dead man's wishes — to be buried without any ceremonies under a stone bench in a little forest clearing.

The sealed gallery is finally to be opened but invitations are not sent out. The dealer intends to do the needful in the presence of the lawyers and yet feels compelled to share that information with some folks who naturally invite themselves. Admirers, fellow-artists, curious locals, excited journalists, art-lovers, casual acquaintances — they are there at the anointed hour.

The lock on the gallery door is rusted. It takes effort and five attempts by three different people to prise it open.

All the lights in the hall are turned on and everyone hurries forward for the first exhilarating glimpse of the dead man's secret. The art dealer tries in vain to advise restrain and hold them back but is roughly pushed aside.

The crowd greedily surges in.

Displayed beautifully on the walls, reflecting the lights, mirror-like, are canvases of different sizes. Untouched by paint, every single canvas is naked and bare.